10/86

Ashfett
Opal

OPAL

By the same author

BEAU BARRON'S LADY
REGENCY ROGUE
THE MICHAELMAS TREE
THE LOVING HIGHWAYMAN
EMERALD
MIDSUMMER-MORNING
PEARL
RUBY
SAPPHIRE

Helen Ashfield
OPAL

St. Martin's Press
New York

OPAL. Copyright © 1986 by Pamela Bennetts. All rights reserved. Printed in the United States of America. No part of this book may be used or reproduced in any manner whatsoever without written permission except in the case of brief quotations embodied in critical articles or reviews. For information, address St. Martin's Press, 175 Fifth Avenue, New York, N.Y. 10010.

Library of Congress Cataloging in Publication Data

Bennetts, Pamela.
  Opal.

  I. Title.
PR6052.E53307 1986   823'.914   86-13020
ISBN 0-312-58591-8

First published in Great Britain by Robert Hale Limited.

First U.S. Edition

10 9 8 7 6 5 4 3 2 1

Acknowledgments

I am deeply grateful to the authors of the following books from which I derived not only information but also much enjoyment. Without their scholarship I would not have been able to write this novel.

The Melody lingers on   W. Macqueen Pope
Life of Charles Morton   H. Chance Newton
Popular Entertainment throughout the Ages   S. McKechnie
Stars Who Made the Halls   S. Théodore Felstead
The Early Doors   Harold Scott
The Music Hall in Britain   D. F. Cheshire
A Hard Act to follow   Peter Leslie
Leisure & Pleasure in the 19C.   Stella Margetson
East End Entertainment   A. E. Wilson
English Night-Life   Thomas Burke
Twice Round the Clock   George Augustus Sala
The Workhouse   Norman Longate
London's Underworld   Henry Mayhew
Handbook of English Costume of the 19C.   C. Willett Cunnington and Phillis Cunnington

OPAL

One

London: 1853

Whatever else might be said about the Shannons, everyone living in the rookery of Raven Court, St. Giles, agreed that they were a close-knit and loving family.

In spite of their own poverty and hardship, the neighbours felt pity for Luke Shannon, blinded in an accident ten years before, and now crippled with arthritis. When he had been hale and hearty he'd had a cheery word for every man, woman and child, and that had never been forgotten.

It was considered that his sons, Hal, sixteen, and Jack, nearly fifteen, tried to be a cut above themselves. Still, whenever there was any real trouble both boys were ready to lend a hand whatever the circumstances.

Em Shannon, a big, blowsy woman with untidy grey hair, ruddy cheeks and a voice like a foghorn, had a heart of gold beating beneath her shabby dress. If anyone fell ill she was there at once with a cup of weak broth or a blanket. Children adored her, clinging about her skirts as she fished in her pocket for a toffee for them. She always seemed to know when a shilling would make the difference between survival and total defeat. The coin was pressed into grateful palms, and the receiver wasn't made to feel a pauper by the gesture. No one asked where Mrs. Shannon obtained such largesse; everyone knew.

If there was a faint murmur of criticism levelled at Em it

was due solely to the fact that she was the most successful pickpocket for miles around. She never came back from her forays empty-handed, and Hal and Jack took after her.

She had trained them carefully. A line was strung across their cramped living-room, an old coat pinned to it. Then she had tucked into its folds a number of bells taken from a child's rattle, placing them cunningly so that they swiftly betrayed any clumsiness.

In no time at all the boys had learned to whisk a handkerchief from the tail-coat pocket, remove a watch, a tiepin, or whatever else their mother had concealed about the garment. Their fingers had become like furtive butterflies, and it wouldn't be long before they were ready to branch out on their own and join the swell mob who hunted richer game.

Opal, aged nine and reed-thin, was the stall, or look-out. She had keen eyes, quick to spot the law or anyone else who was casting a dubious glance at the gang as they went about their nefarious business. She wasn't proud of what she did, knowing it was wholly wrong. However, as her mother had pointed out, it was that or starving.

"Wouldn't want your pa to go without his victuals, would you?" she asked once when Opal had demurred at accompanying her. "'E cared for us when 'e could and now it's our turn to see to 'im. I'm not clever like some, luv. Can't sew or nothin' like that. This is the only way I know 'ow to keep 'im warm and fed, and you lot too. You do see, don't you?"

Opal had given her mother a hug and said no more. Em was right; Luke Shannon, huddled in his chair, did need their help, and she had enough sense in her head to see that there was no other way of getting money, at least for the time being.

On the morning of Christmas Eve the Shannons and Miss Polly Jones, their lodger, sat round the table and discussed their plan of action. Polly had once been a governess but had fallen on hard times. Em had discovered her weeping in an alley, a dead, day-old baby in her arms.

After that, Polly shared the Shannon's two rooms, keeping the place as clean as she could. It wasn't easy. The floor was oozing with damp, the windows broken and stuffed with paper to keep out the draughts. The furniture was falling to pieces, and hungry rats had to be driven away almost hourly.

But Miss Jones's gratitude hadn't stopped at her efforts with a bucket and mop. She had taken to Opal at once, pleading with Mrs. Shannon to let her teach the child to read and write. Em hadn't minded. Indeed, she was rather proud that at least one of her fledglings would have some education. Opal's mind was as sharp as her eye, and she had proved a hard-working and dedicated pupil. The tutoring hadn't been confined to reading and writing. Opal could add, multiply and subtract, knew something of history and geography, and could even speak a few words of French.

"I think we'll go to Regent Street this afternoon," said Em reflectively. "Bound to be a big crowd there. They'll all be thinkin' of what they're goin' to buy. Won't notice us at all, I don't suppose."

"Bit of a risk, ma." Hal lounged back in a chair which threatened to give way under him. "Never been to the West End before, 'ave we?"

"No reason why we can't go today. You and Jack 'ave got them tweed trousers which don't look bad, and the jackets and boots you pinched last week. You'll not stand out too much, 'specially if you keep movin'."

"What about you?"

Em looked sly at Jack's question.

"Ah well. I didn't tell you at the time, but I got myself quite a decent dress not long since. Been savin' it up for summat like this. Reckon if I put some o' that red ribbon I nicked round me bonnet I could pass for a countrywoman up to see the sights."

"What about Opal, my dear?"

Luke had a gentle voice, like his nature. Before tragedy struck him he had been a singer in an East End tavern. It hadn't paid all that well. Just a few shillings a week, his food, and a pint or two of ale. When he wasn't singing he had humped sacks and crates in the local market. His total earnings hadn't been much, but somehow they'd got by.

Now he had to rely on Em and his sons, but they never made him feel a burden. Like Opal, he hated what his wife did, but he accepted that there was no choice. To have chided her would have made her lot worse, and he would never knowingly have hurt his Em.

Mrs. Shannon turned to smile at her husband, although she knew he couldn't see her. She still loved him as much as on the day that she had married him. No one realised that beneath her breezy manner and coarse humour she often cried in her heart for what the two of them had lost.

"Got summat for 'er, too. Pretty dress, even if it is a bit worn in places. It's blue, same as 'er eyes, and she'll look like a princess in it."

"And I've got a sash put by." Polly was anxious to do her bit. "Funny thing, but that's blue as well. Didn't know what I was hoarding it for, but now I do."

Opal felt quite excited. The prospect of something different to wear and a trip to the West End had driven the purpose of their jaunt from her mind for a while.

She was thinking of the adventure ahead as Em and the others discussed the details of their campaign. She hardly heard her mother's cautionary words as to the kind of man or woman who would make the best mark. She was dwelling on the thought of the blue dress, and the sash which Polly was going to give her.

When they got to Regent Street at about four o'clock, Opal was stunned. Never in her wildest dreams had she pictured anything so magnificent, and her mouth opened in silent disbelief.

The shops were so big, with vast plate-glass windows brilliantly lit. There were gowns of silk and satin, cloaks with embroidered collars and beads round their hems. In one store cascades of cobweb lace, as white as the snow which had just started to fall, were draped over a silver rod next to curling ostrich feathers and sable muffs.

There were places selling reticules, parasols, fine suède gloves and shoes of expensive, supple leather. Shawls of every hue, silk-fringed, lay cheek by jowl with fans spread out like the tails of proud peacocks. In the jewellers' shops there were glittering gems, and clocks in gold and silver cases which ticked away the hours.

But the final wonder was the Christmas tree. It stood in a bow-fronted window, illuminated by a myriad of tiny tapers, and from its branches were suspended small, exciting gifts and mouth-watering sugar-plums. Luke had once told her that they were also called Trees of Love. She had thought it a beautiful name, but had never expected to see one in all its glory.

She was hardly conscious of the shoppers hurrying to and fro, or of the carriages, hansom cabs and four-wheelers which raced down Nash's elegant thoroughfare.

"Look, ma," she said finally. "Isn't it wonderful? I've never seen anything like it before."

Em was dry.

"Nay, and I don't suppose you'll see such a thing again, leastways, not in Raven Court. Come on, ducks. Jack's just seen a likely couple. The old girl's got up to the nines and there's a smart young gent with her. Probably easier to lift his wallet than take her purse. Keep your eyes peeled, won't you? We've done well so far. Don't want to spoil things now."

Blissfully unaware of what was about to happen, Annice, Dowager Duchess of Ware, was examining some crystal glasses in Davis's window, wondering if they would do for her cousin Bella. As Em had said, she did look grand, with a Parisian hat perched on her head and furs round her shoulders.

Annice always came to London to spend the festive season with her daughter and son-in-law, the Earl and Countess of

Kynston. It was also a chance to see her grandchildren on whom she doted and spoilt quite outrageously.

She hated town and left her arrival until the last minute. No sooner had she supervised the unloading of her luggage than she was demanding that a carriage be made ready to take her to Regent Street. She had no intention of going alone, and everyone knew it. Edward Adare, Viscount Peverell, was her favourite grandson, and it was accepted that his task was to accompany her on her shopping spree. It was all part of the Christmas ritual.

Edward was fourteen and very sophisticated for his age. He teased his grandmother wickedly and called her Annie as a pet name. His insolence was taken in good part, and forgiven, for it was all done with much love.

Besides, Edward reminded Annice of someone she had known a long time ago. In spite of his youth, the viscount had all of the charm and good looks of the duchesses beau. Sometimes when he turned his head Annice felt a qualm run through her, for it was almost as if the man in question had come back to her.

She often told Edward that one day he would be a heart-breaker. He scoffed at the notion, having no time for the opposite sex. Girls, he told his grandmother, were silly creatures and not worth a moment's consideration.

He didn't mind going with Her Grace. As he had only returned from Eton that morning he had his own gifts to buy. In any event, being with Annie was fun and he had every intention of enjoying himself.

They had brought with them the duchess's personal maid, Doris Whicker, and Simpson and Loomis, two of the earl's footmen who were to carry the parcels. Somehow the small entourage had got split up in the mêlée, but Annice hardly noticed that.

"No, they're far too dear," she said, turning away from Davis's emporium. "It's a ridiculous price to ask."

Peverell was trying to hang on to his hat with one hand and guide the duchess with the other. The pavement was growing slippery and Annice wasn't as young as she had been, nor her foot so sure.

"You can afford it," he said with a grin. "You're as rich as Croesus."

"How do you know, you impudent young whippersnapper?"

"You told me so."

"Did I? I must be losing my wits. Anyway, I don't like Bella, so she'll get something costing a great deal less than those wine goblets."

"I hope you're not going to economise on my present."

"What makes you think I'm going to give you one?"

Peverell laughed and kissed her.

"You will, you always do. I hope it's a horse."

"You're horse mad." The duchess assumed a crossness she didn't feel. It was almost as if her lost love had touched her cheek. "And you can't do things like that in public."

"Yes I can. I'm starting a new fashion."

He didn't hear the duchess's tart response because suddenly he was aware that someone was pressing close to his back. When he turned there was no one special in view or even very near to him. There was just a sea of faces and the chatter of voices high-lighted with laughter. Then he saw the girl.

She stood a few paces away from him, small, slight, with hair as golden as a guinea and the largest blue eyes he had ever seen. She was plainly dressed and obviously poor, for her shoes were scuffed, her skirt patched. He could see that she was shivering from the cold and, absurdly, wanted to take off his coat and put it round her.

"Edward! Are you listening to me?"

The viscount came down to earth with a bump.

"No, I'm sorry. What did you say?"

"Really! You're every bit as bad as your grandfather was. He never paid any attention to me when I took him shopping. I asked if you had enough money left to buy your mother some perfume."

Edward reached for his pocket-book, not in the least surprised to find it was no longer there. Pickpocketing was a scourge to which everyone was prey, and then he knew why he had felt the presence of another behind him.

It was obvious that the child in blue had been with the felon; she didn't belong in Regent Street at all, never mind on her own. He felt a pang of disappointment because he didn't want to think of her as a thief.

He raised his head, hoping she wasn't as pretty as he'd thought, but she had gone, swallowed up in the crowd.

When the duchess realised what had happened she made a great to-do, ignoring her grandson's plea to let matters rest. Whicker and the two footmen had struggled through the ever-increasing throng to join Annice, who promptly despatched Loomis to find a constable.

"Give those packages to Whicker," she commanded imperiously. "The viscount's been robbed and I want the villain apprehended. Go on, man, be off with you."

Loomis looked at the duchess helplessly. There was not the slightest chance of finding the culprit, but he knew better than to argue with Her Grace. He pushed his load on to Doris, who promptly dropped the lot.

"You idiotic woman!" Annice was more than usually acid, for in truth she was growing tired and didn't want to admit it. "Pick those things up at once, and if anything's broken you'll pay for it."

Edward helped to rescue the purchases, quite unmoved by his grandmother's empty threat. Annice's bark was ferocious, but she was the kindest creature on earth. He was one of the very few people who knew that the duchess paid Whicker twice the normal wage because the maid had an invalid mother and a dying sister to support.

As he straightened up he saw the girl coming towards him again. She thrust the pocket-book into his hand without a word, and he was thankful that Annice and Doris were still too busy with their parcels to notice what was happening.

Opal had taken one look at the tall, comely boy and had

fallen in love. She thought the way his dark hair curled slightly under his top hat was miraculous, and that his clear hazel eyes were as bright as any of the jewellers' wares. His nose was thin and high-bridged, making him look a trifle severe until one noticed the smile lurking round the corners of his mouth.

She had pleaded hard with Em.

"Ma, let me give it back to him. We've got enough already."

Mrs. Shannon had stared at her daughter in disbelief.

"Give it back? Are you goin' soft in the 'ead? There's five pounds in it, and the rent's four weeks behind. 'Ad to buy another blanket for yer father, so Mr. Jobb's got to wait for 'is money."

"There are others who look just as wealthy. We can try again, can't we?"

"Why should we?"

"Oh please, please! Don't let's keep this one."

"I don't see – "

"Ma! I'll do anything you ask – anything. Just this once let me do what I want. It'll be as if you're giving me a Christmas present."

Em had opened her mouth to put Opal firmly in her place and to tell her not to be such a blamed fool when she saw the look in her daughter's eyes. Opal was only nine, but the expression was unmistakable. She'd seen the same awe in herself when she'd looked in a mirror during her courtship with Luke. She hesitated and was lost.

"What'll the boys say?"

"Nothing, if you tell them you dropped it somewhere."

"They knows I never drop anything."

"You could have done this time, what with all these people barging into you. You could pretend you slipped. It's snowing quite hard now."

Reluctantly Mrs. Shannon had handed over the wallet. It would mean extra work, finding someone who looked equally well-endowed, but she'd manage somehow. The joy in Opal made up for the inconvenience. Hal and Jack might raise their eyebrows if they found out, but they knew they'd get a clip round the ear if they sauced her.

"All right, 'ere you are. You won't never see 'im no more, you know."

Opal and her mother shared the secret for a second or two.

"No, I know, but it doesn't matter. I'll remember him."

" 'Spect you will. All women are balmy that way. Go on then, look lively and git it over with. We've other things to do afore we goes 'ome."

When Opal found Edward again she began to tremble, and not only because of the biting wind.

"Thank you," he said softly. "I'm very grateful."

She couldn't find words to answer him, flushing in a way which made him marvel anew. He'd never studied a girl's face so closely before and his head was spinning slightly as well. They just stood and gazed at each other for a moment; then Opal ran.

"Where is that wretched policeman?" Annice had finished with Whicker and the gaily-wrapped gifts with their bows of satin ribbon. "We could all be murdered by footpads standing about like this."

Edward gave a deep sigh. It was over, that fleeting and remarkable encounter, and he was sad. He would like to have talked to the small stranger and asked her name. Now he never could. She had gone out of his life for good.

"I don't think there are any footpads in Regent Street nowadays," he said with a faint laugh. "And we don't need a policeman either. Someone has just given me back my pocket-book. I must have dropped it when I pulled out my handkerchief."

Annice's ear was finely attuned to every shade of Edward's voice and she had never heard that particular note before. She frowned, sensing danger.

"Someone? What sort of someone?"

"Just a girl."

"On her own?"

"She seemed to be. She was very young."

"Then she's probably robbed you. Have a look."

Peverell didn't really want to, but to object would increase the risk of more questions which he couldn't answer.

"No, the note is still here," he said finally. "She didn't take it."

He wondered why she hadn't. She was obviously in need of money, and just some of what she had returned to him would have bought her warm clothes and food. He hoped that she wouldn't get into trouble with those who must have been with her. The thought that the child might be beaten for her unexpected honesty disturbed him.

"Just as well." Annice still wasn't satisfied, but one day she'd wheedle out of her grandson the reason why he'd looked as he did. "All right, let's get on or we'll still be here at midnight. Simpson, go and find Loomis and then the pair of you go to the Haymarket and wait by the carriage. If you're not there by the time I'm ready to leave you'll have to walk home. Whicker, stop sniffing and mind where you're putting your feet. We don't want any more accidents."

Edward gave Simpson a sympathetic grimace and then turned to the matter in hand.

"I suppose you don't know what kind of scent mother likes?"

"Of course I do, and so should you. A man ought to know which perfume the women in his life use, and what size their – oh never mind. You're not old enough for that yet."

"Spoil-sport."

"Perhaps, but you're far too precocious as it is. Now, here we are, this is the counter. Pay close attention and don't start daydreaming again. This is going to be your first lesson in how to please a woman, and, believe me, you'll never learn anything more useful than that if you live to be a hundred."

* * *

The remainder of Christmas Eve was a busy one for Em and her family. First, Em had been to see the local receiver, Abel Schumann, and spent twenty minutes arguing with him over the value of the tie-pins, watches, brooches and handkerchiefs laid on his counter.

Em hadn't found the pocket-book returned by Opal a problem. She had managed to filch another from an elderly gentleman tottering along the kerb trying to attract the attention of a hansom-cabby. Hal and Jack hadn't seen her at work, assuming the note was from Jack's original dip.

After Mr. Schumann came the trip to *The Thirsty Hound* public house near Raven Court. It was from there that the Goose Club was run, and even the very poorest of people managed to put a few coppers into the kitty during the year so that roast goose would grace their tables on Christmas Day.

Then off to the market where Hal whipped a leg of mutton off its hook, neat as you please, when Jack created a diversion by tipping the butcher's hat over his eyes.

Em used most of her ill-gotten gains to buy presents, ignoring the rent arrears. She bought a new jacket and trousers for Luke, smugly paying cash, but whipping a shirt under her apron as the stall-holder turned to wrap up her purchases.

She didn't intend to pay for any food or drink; they would be furnished by other means. That left her enough for a blouse for Polly and a thick shawl for Opal. Seeing her money was running low, she meandered casually up to a booth where cheap watches were being sold. As the vendor waxed enthusiastic over the one Em held in her left hand, her right hand dextrously appropriated two of its fellows for the boys.

Jack wasn't going to let Hal be the only one to help furnish the table. He managed to half-fill a sack with potatoes, carrots and rosy-cheeked apples, the harassed greengrocer to busy arguing with a woman who was complaining about the quality of his oranges to notice that he was being robbed. Moving on, he collected a bag of sugar, some tea, a plum cake and a bag of sweets. Em, not to be outdone, helped herself to a bottle of gin and some tobacco from the baskets of unsuspecting shoppers.

When they got home, Polly had a good fire burning in the grate and had spent some of the hard-earned money she got from sewing and washing on sprigs of holly and mistletoe. She had cleaned the room thoroughly, laying dry sacking on the floor, and had made the cheap plates and cups on the dresser shine like best porcelain.

"Did you do well, dear?"

Luke always asked. It was only fair, whatever he thought of Em's activities. If it hadn't been for her he would be in the workhouse.

"That we did." Em gave him a smacking kiss on his cheek. "As to the bird, why it's so plump it'll melt in the mouth afore you can taste it."

"Regent Street was marvellous, pa." Opal snuggled down beside her father, eager to impart all her impressions. "It was so full of colour and light. I saw a Tree of Love, too."

The word 'love' made Mrs. Shannon glance down at her daughter. Silly to fuss over a child of that age, but she made herself a promise there and then. Opal would never go to the West End again, not while she, Em, had anything to say about it. No use the girl pining for something she could never have. In future she would stay in the neighbourhood of St. Giles where she belonged.

"Now, who's going to take the goose to Mr. Edman in the morning?" she asked, dismissing the worry from her mind. "Hal or you, Jack?"

Edman was the local baker. His shop stayed open on Christmas Day, but not only to sell fresh bread. Like his fellow-bakers he kept his ovens alight so that his customers could bring their poultry to be cooked. Their own fires, if they had any, weren't up to such a task.

"I'll go, ma." Jack was smoking a generous stub of cigar

he'd found in the gutter. "Make sure I'm awake early, though."

"That I will, and you're too young to be doin' that. Give it to yer pa. 'Ere, Luke, a nice bit o' fancy baccy for yer. Opal, help Polly to lay the table. I'm fair wore out, and a nice bit o' cold pie I rescued on the way 'ome will go down a fair treat. Hal, git the cups. We ain't got glasses like we saw this afternoon, but gin's gin whatever yer drinks it out of."

Christmas dinner was a great success. As Em had predicted her goose was moist and tender, its skin crisp and golden brown. Polly had quite a way with roast potatoes, and she had made a pudding wrapped in a cloth and hung over the fire in an iron pot. It was full of fruit, nuts and treacle, for which she'd saved hard, and was rich to the palate.

"Don't know 'ow you does it, Pol," said Mrs. Shannon appreciatively, for she had a sweet tooth. "Best you've made yet."

Polly bridled with pleasure, stroking the lace on her new blouse and feeling like a queen.

They lingered over the meal. It was the one day in the year on which they didn't have to hurry, and they made the most of it. When at last they were replete to the point of bursting, and the pots had been washed in the sink and left to drain, Em stretched her arms above her head.

"Well, that's better, ain't it? Now what'll we do next?"

Everyone laughed, for they all knew what was coming. It was Luke's special time, and they settled down round the fire to roast chestnuts and listen to his tales of the old taverns, the penny gaffs, the song and supper-rooms and the new up-and-coming music halls.

Shannon's friends hadn't forgotten him after his accident. They often popped in to see him, regaling him with all the latest gossip and singing new songs which were popular with their audiences.

Mrs. Shannon and the others had heard it many times before, but it gave Luke such pleasure to talk of times past and present that none of them begrudged him one minute of their attention.

He began, as he always did, with the way in which men had once liked a sing-song in ancient ale-houses and inns, and later in the tap-rooms of public houses. From such small beginnings had grown song and supper-rooms and places like the notorious Cyder Cellar in Maiden Lane, and the Coal Hole. The latter two had been the haunts of the fashionable bucks of the eighteenth century, and Luke was careful to draw a veil over some of the wickednesses which had gone on in them.

"Tell us about Evans's Song and Supper-Room, pa." Opal loved to listen to her father and never tired of the details. She fully intended to follow in his footsteps and then become a star of the music halls. She wasn't going to spend the rest of her life stealing if she could help it and was eager to drink in every word Luke uttered. "Right from the beginning."

Shannon ruffled her hair with an affectionate hand. He knew quite well that the others were merely indulging him, but his daughter's enthusiasm was genuine. He was also aware of her aspirations and encouraged them. He wanted her to be a success, and anything would be better than his baby being a buzzer when she grew up.

"Well, it all started in 1840 when Mr. Evans bought a nobleman's mansion in Covent Garden. He made a great dining-hall where men could eat the finest food and drink wine as they listened to the professional entertainers he had hired. The place was a success from the word go."

Em dozed through the long tale of the birth of the music hall. She knew all about the progression from free-and-easies, penny gaffs, and glee-clubs to the modern palaces of delight fit for a monarch.

She had also heard of Charles Morton, whose name popped up frequently in Luke's story. Morton had bought the old *Canterbury Arms* over Lambeth way and made it the wonder of everyone who patronised it. She had a soft spot for the entrepreneur, although she'd never seen him. He had been the first to welcome women to his hall as well as men, and had created history by making a charge for the entertainment alone. Others of his kind still sold tickets for food and drink and threw the amusements in free gratis. Charles Morton, as everyone agreed, was the father of the true music hall.

She roused when Luke began to sing. It made tears come into her eyes for all that it was a jolly ditty, intended to make the hearers laugh. Luke had real talent, but now he was just a carcass, unable to move without aid.

The arthritis was growing worse, and Em could have wept when he apologised to her because he couldn't wash himself. She scolded him with a false roughness for being so foolish, but she knew only too well what the loss of such basic dignity had done to him.

She stopped snivelling when it was Opal's turn. Her maternal pride glowed fiercely as her daughter sang in a sweet, true voice. Opal wasn't as expert as her father, but she had a good many years to learn how to use her gift. The trouble was that so many wanted to get themselves into the mushrooming music halls. There wasn't going to be much of a hope for a shrimp of a child from a rookery, clad in near-rags.

Em wished she'd saved some of the money she'd got by her thieving. There hadn't really been all that much to spare, of course. There was the rent, which had to be paid sometimes if they weren't to be evicted, and food to buy when it couldn't be obtained by sleight of hand. She kept a fire burning night and day for her husband, and none of her children had ever gone bare-foot or had their bottoms hanging out of their trousers. Still, she should have tried to set something aside.

As Opal finished, Em made a resolution. In the New Year she would start to save, and not just for the Christmas goose. She'd put the coppers somewhere safe, in case there was ever a chance for Opal, who'd need a decent outfit to make an impression.

Opal acknowledged her family's applause with a blush. She was thinking of the boy in Regent Street, for whom she had really sung her melody, although he couldn't hear it.

Her mother had been right. They wouldn't see each other again, but every line of his face was imprinted on her mind. When she was low and unhappy she would be able to conjure up his image, and the smile he had given her would provide all the comfort needed. Maybe she had only seen him once, but it was enough.

For better or worse he would be with her for the rest of her days, and she went over to Em and put her arms round her, silently thanking her for the best Christmas present she had ever had.

Two

Em Shannon didn't have the chance to keep her resolve about saving for the future.

Early in February she and Opal had gone to fetch water, waiting an interminable time at the stand-pipe round the corner for the supply to be turned on. When they hurried back to Raven Court, slipping and sliding on the ice, they saw the fire.

It was an inferno, greedy flames shooting up to the dark sky, clouds of smoke billowing out of doors and windows. They knew at once that their home was engulfed in the raging horror. Opal screamed, but Em, white to the lips, merely mouthed Luke's name as she ran forward.

Neighbours held them back. No one could save the occupants trapped in the conflagration. They were cut off from would-be rescuers by a wall more solid than stone.

When it was all over, six houses lay ruined and open to the elements. Mrs. Toppit, Em's friend, said that Hal and Jack had darted into the tenement to try to get their father and Polly out, but neither were seen again. The fire had been rapacious and consumed anyone venturing into its heart.

After that Em appeared to lose the will to live. She and the stricken Opal still stayed in the wreckage; there wasn't anywhere else for them to go. However much people wanted to give them succour their own houses were jam-packed.

When it rained or snowed, Opal and Em got wet. When the east wind curled itself cruelly through the shell they turned blue. Food was scarce. Mrs. Shannon's hands shook so much that there was no chance of her taking anything without being caught. Besides, she didn't seem to want to. She wasn't hungry herself and appeared oblivious to her daughter's needs.

Opal understood. She blamed herself for not having learned the lessons which Hal and Jack had done. It was she who ought to have gone out foraging, but she didn't know how to set about the task.

Inevitably, Em fell ill. She lay supine, burning with fever, murmuring words of endearment which Opal knew were meant for her father. One day when Mrs. Toppit picked her way over charred wood with a bottle of tea and some stale bread, Opal was told to go outside for a while. She rebelled at first, but Em got so upset she had to obey in the end.

"You can go back now, pet," said Ena Toppit as she hugged her shawl about her. "Get yourself a nice hot drink, and, duckie – "

"Yes?"

Ena's courage failed her at the last moment

"Ain't nothing. Go and see to yer ma."

When Em had taken a disinterested sip or two of tea she said in a whisper:

"Best I tell you straight what's goin' to 'appen, luv."

Opal forgot the piece of bread in her hand, her heart suddenly starting to thump.

"Happen? Why nothing's going to happen, 'cept you're going to get well and then we'll be finding another place."

Mrs. Shannon gave a sigh which seemed to come from what was left of her boots.

"No, I'm not goin' to git better. Wish – wish I could, for your sake, but I'm done for."

"No, ma!"

" 'Fraid so. Don't care for meself; it'll be nice to be with Luke again."

"But – "

"Listen, girl, for I don't think there's much time left."

Em's voice was a faint whisper. " 'Aven't been able – able to git me breath back proper this last hour. When I'm – I'm gorn, you'll be on yer own. Can't – can't leave it like that." There was a long pause while Em fought for air. "You won't be able to fend for yerself and Gawd knows what 'ud 'appen to you if yer roamed the streets."

The words were barely audible now, and Opal crouched close fighting back tears as her mother went on.

"I've asked Mrs. Toppit to call them at the – the workhouse. Not what I wanted for yer, but you'll 'ave a roof over yer 'ead and – and summat – summat to eat."

"Not the workhouse!" Opal shrank back as if she'd been struck. "You can't send me there – not to Lockgate."

"I'll – I'll 'ave to. Won't be so bad, you'll see."

"It will, it will! Everyone says the House is a ghastly place. They beat you there and shut you in cupboards if you're bad. Jack told me so."

For a moment Opal thought her mother was too far gone to hear her, but somehow Em made one last effort.

" 'Ow would 'e know. 'E'd never – never been inside."

"George Wass told him. Ma, please, please don't make me go there. I'll run away, rather than that."

"And break me 'eart?"

Mrs. Shannon's dull eyes met her daughter's as tears began to trickle down her cheeks.

"Let me go peaceful, there's a good 'un. Couldn't rest in me grave if I thought yer weren't bein' cared for. Say – say you'll go, when they come for you. Oh, luv, say you will!"

Dully Opal gave her promise, a terrible fear closing in on her. George Wass's tale wasn't the only one she'd heard about the much-dreaded Lockgate. But she couldn't deny her mother a quiet passing, and so she nodded.

"All right, ma, don't upset yourself. You rest now."

The sick woman lapsed into a fretful sleep, but after an hour or so the struggle was over and the rattle in Em's throat stilled. Opal stared down at her mother's waxen face, totally numb. She couldn't imagine what it was going to be like without Em, who had been a tower of strength simply by existing. Even as she had lain dying there had been something indomitable about her.

Opal got to her feet and walked out into the cobbled yard. Mrs. Toppit and her two daughters were there, ready to give what help they could.

"How long will it be before they come for me?" asked Opal when she had swallowed her own tears. "Will it be soon?"

"Aye, not long. Come in with us for a bit and get warm. Don't let it get you down, will you?"

Opal gave Ena a very adult look, the last of childhood falling away from her.

"No, Mrs. Toppit, I won't. I hope ma can hear me because I'm going to fight for her sake. No matter what the House is like, I won't let it beat me. Nothing's ever going to do that, and that's a promise."

* * *

The new Poor Law had decreed that all parishes in the country were to be merged and then divided into a number of unions. Each was to have a body to run it, elected by those who paid rates, and committees were to be known as Guardians of the Poor.

Out-relief was only given to the old and helpless poor. Everyone else who was destitute found themselves in what was the central core of each union, the local workhouse.

Lockgate was typical of its kind. Opal stared in dismay at the squat, three-storied building with lower wings on each side of it. It looked like a prison, and for the young it was just that. Their elders might try again in the outside world, but children who ran away were brought back and punished with severity.

The god-like creature who ran Lockgate was the Workhouse Master, a surly, unfeeling man called Gregg who had once served in the army. To help him, there was the

Clerk of the Union, a matron, a chaplain who called once a week to minister to the souls of those incarcerated, and a medical officer who was seldom sober.

In addition to these illustrious officers, there were two cooks and a number of assistants, as heartless and brutal as their overlord.

Opal's first shock upon entering Lockgate was to be herded with a group of other girls of her own age into a dank room with water running down the walls. There they were stripped of their own clothes, washed in icy water, and made to sit on a plank with splinters in it whilst their hair was cropped close to their skulls.

That done, each new arrival was given drawers, a shift, and a dress of thick woollen stuff, badly made and abrasive on the skin. The hobnailed boots had heavy metal tips, and it felt to Opal as though her feet were weighted to the floor. It didn't take her long to learn about the remainder of Lockgate's iron regime either.

The dormitories were crowded with cheap wooden beds, each having a lumpy flock mattress and a blanket, the smell of which made Opal retch. Often beds had to be shared, and the stench of sweat and worse, together with bugs, fleas and cockroaches, quite convinced Opal that she was already in hell.

The food was doled out sparingly, the children getting less than men and women. Watery gruel, bread, a bit of hard cheese, and an occasional potato was the normal diet. There was nothing hot to drink, tea being forbidden to all but the very old. The water smelt of drains, and often Opal went thirsty rather than let the noxious stuff go down her throat.

Hours were long; up at five in the morning in summer, seven in winter. Work started after prayers and breakfast and lasted until supper at six. All the inmates were in bed by eight, most falling asleep at once through sheer exhaustion.

The men picked oakum, made sacks, or ground bones to be sold as fertiliser, whilst the children scrubbed and cleaned and then sat about their cell-like room, apathetic, tired, and starving.

Opal was praying that she could die when one day she was moved to another section of the House and met Davey Campbell, fourteen, and Susie Phelps, aged eight.

No one had given her a second look since she had got to Lockgate, never mind bestowing a smile on her. But Davey gave her a friendly grin, and shy, pretty Susie offered her a tentative greeting.

Davey proved his mettle two days after Opal had arrived on the block. One of the older boys had tried to rape her. She had struggled as hard as she could, but she knew she was losing the battle. Then Davey had come and suddenly she was free, her molester beaten half to death before two assistants had rushed in to rescue him.

Campbell had been flogged and shut up in a store for three days without food, but had emerged as defiant and as spirited as ever.

"One day I'll repay you, Davey," Opal had said earnestly. "I promise I will."

"No need for that."

"Yes there is. It's important to me. I'm going to give you my solemn oath that if ever you're in trouble when we get out of this place I'll help you."

He'd laughed at her, but not unkindly, pleased by her obvious respect, and after that no one had dared to give her even a black look.

With Davey and Susie for company things got better. The workhouse didn't change, but Opal had two friends and that made all the difference. They exchanged their histories, Opal finding that Davey's and Susie's were just as sad as her own. Their common condition bound them together as tightly as a blood-tie. They were a new family for her and she thanked God for His mercy.

Although she told Davey and Susie all about Em, Luke and her brothers, she didn't mention the boy in Regent Street. He was hers exclusively and reserved for dreams. As she had expected, the thought of him and the smile he had given her did bring consolation. He provided her with a reserve of courage when things got too bad.

When there was time she spoke of her desire to go on the halls. Davey and Susie listened avidly to Luke's reminiscences, for they'd never heard anything so exciting in the whole of their drab lives.

"And I'll be a star myself one day," said Opal when their labours were over and they had found a comparatively quiet corner in which to sit. "I'm going to sing and dance."

Davey Campbell had copper-coloured hair, grey eyes and a square-cut jaw. He wasn't handsome like Opal's young man. Nevertheless, she found him attractive, not least because of his strength of purpose and physical prowess which kept the other inmates in their places.

"Can you sing?" Davey was leaning against the wall, unravelling a piece of rope. "Ever done anything like that in public?"

"I can sing, but only my family heard me."

"Same with dancing, I suppose?"

"I'm sure you do both beautifully," said Susie quickly, afraid that Opal might be hurt by Davey's scepticism. "Don't tease, Davey."

Opal smiled at her champion. The latter had big dark eyes and would have had curls to match had not her locks been snipped away until she looked almost bald. She leaned on Davey for help and support, and had soon turned to Opal as well when she could see her friend's stoicism was as firm as Campbell's. Susie was one of life's victims, and, without a word being exchanged between them, Opal and Davey took on the task of protecting the fragile child.

"I don't mind him. I'm good, I know I am. I'll get what I want in the end."

Davey nodded. He had similar ambitions, but his future plans had nothing to do with entertainment. He wanted money and intended to get it in any way he could. He had a fair idea of the best way to go about things. People needed food. When they were hungry they had to pay for bread and suchlike. He would start with a barrow and then get a stall. After that it would be a shop and, later, other shops, until he had a whole string of them. Folk needed somewhere to live as well. Buying up derelict property and letting it at exhorbitant rents was another method of accumulating wealth. He was going to try anything and everything which would get him where he wanted to go.

"Give us a tune now, then."

Opal turned to look at him.

"What here – now?"

He mocked her.

"Why not? 'Fraid we'll see you're a sham?"

"No, of course not, and I'm not a sham. I'll shew you, Davey Campbell. You're not the only one who wants to get on."

Susie was frightened, begging Opal not to pick up the gauntlet.

"They'll shut you in The Death Hole," she whispered, her face paling at the mere thought of it. "The other day one of the assistants caught Sammy Henton whistling. He got locked up for six hours and he said it was awful. The people in there aren't really dead. They move about and touch anyone who disturbs them with bony fingers. Oh please don't! Davey, it isn't fair to make her."

"I'm not making her." Campbell gave Opal a glance from under lowered lids. He quite fancied the girl whose eyes looked like deep blue pools, but he wanted to see her mettle. He'd no time for cowards however lovely they were. "It's up to her. She says she can sing and dance. I say we've got to see her do it before we can believe her."

In the middle of one of the songs Luke had taught her Opal began to dance as well. Others clustered round, amazed by the spectacle. They were filled with admiration, too. Like Campbell, they knew what price she would have to pay if the door opened suddenly.

Opal's luck was out. She was nearing the end of the last verse when a heavy hand fell on her shoulder, her companions scattering like dried leaves in the wind. Only Davey remained, standing straight as if he wanted to thrust himself between her and May Crooker, the most unpleasant of all the assistants in Lockgate.

But there was nothing Davey could do. Opal was dragged out by the scruff of her neck, down long stone corridors and flights of worn steps to a room which was always kept locked.

"You little cow." Crooker was glad to have found someone she could punish with real justification. "I'll teach you to mess about like that."

Opal tried to free herself and got a hard thump for doing so.

"I was only singing. There's nothing wrong with that."

"There's everything wrong with it in here, and don't you answer me back. You'll spend the night in The Hole, you hoity-toity miss. See how you get on yowling and throwing your arms and legs about in front of them corpses. Perhaps they'll enjoy it and clap, who knows?"

"You're not allowed to shut us in here. It's against the rules."

May looked in Opal's stormy eyes and saw no fear. There was just anger and contempt, and her blood boiled over.

"Oh, so now you know all about the rules, do you? Not here a full three months, but you know more about how things run here than I do after fifteen years. You bloody bitch, I'll make you think twice before you cheek me again."

The attendants always carried a wooden stick fixed to their belts, and Opal found herself seized by the buxom Crooker who had a grip of iron. She didn't cry out, but her lip was bleeding as the door was opened and she was thrown headlong inside.

It was icily still in there when the key had turned in the lock. Opal picked herself up and felt her heart flutter as she looked round. There was one small vent near the ceiling which let in some air to off-set the smell of death, but it also shed light on the five bodies stretched out on boards, naked except for a piece of sacking over the lower part of their torsos.

In that first minute Opal knew that the supreme test for her future life had come. She could cringe under the table and listen to her own teeth chattering as she waited for the touch of the hand of which Susie had spoken. The alternative was to thumb a nose at May Crooker and all the cruelty exercised within Lockgate's walls. To stand up, despite the bruises, and let the dead and living know that she wasn't going to fall at the first fence.

Slowly she began to move, catching the hem of her torn frock as she swayed to and fro. Then came the song, her notes pitched as high as a lark's and twice as pure. When her performance was finished she looked back at the corpses. They didn't frighten her any more. They'd just been poor, sick people who had probably been glad to die.

She put her hands on her hips and smiled grimly at the door.

"Well, Madam Crooker?" she asked out loud. "What did you think of that? You and your stick and your Death Hole aren't going to stop me. Why don't you come on in, you old harridan? I'm just about to do an encore."

* * *

Opal rejoined those on Block A just after the others had finished their midday meal.

The bread was harder than ever that day, the sliver of cheese more rancid. Susie Phelps couldn't eat a thing. She had been crying most of the night because of her fears for Opal, and even Davey Campbell was quiet.

He had a very uneasy conscience about Opal. He had egged the girl on, simply to see what stuff she was made of. He hadn't stopped to think about Susie's warning and what the mortuary was really like. He had slept fitfully, starting awake every so often, picturing Opal in the cold and darkness.

He even wondered if it would affect her mind. Certainly she would be hysterical when she was released and would probably have nightmares for months to come.

When he saw Opal walk into the room he felt a sense of sharp relief. Her chin was up, her eyes unafraid, her hands as steady as a rock as she closed the door behind her.

"Never did finish that song, did I?" she asked calmly. "Well, here goes; this is the last chorus."

They all watched open-mouthed as she did a couple of pirouettes and chanted the words defiantly. No one else had ever come out of The Death Hole looking like Opal Shannon did and certainly none had repeated the misdeeds which had put them there in the first place.

She was their heroine from that moment onwards. Susie wept in her arms until Opal laughed and shook her gently.

"Come on, Susie, you're more miserable than that lot in The Hole. At least they didn't interrupt me when I was singing."

Davey drew Opal aside when Susie was satisfied that no harm had come to her friend.

"Did you really sing in there?"

He was very offhand, concealing his esteem. Wouldn't do for her to get swollen headed, but she was a real corker and no mistake.

" 'Course I did; danced as well. Didn't get much of a hand for my trouble, but it was all good practice."

"Weren't you – didn't they bother you?"

He still hesitated a little, waiting to see if her bravado was a veneer spread over terror.

"The bodies? No, why should they? They didn't whack me like Old Mother Crooker did."

Campbell's mouth turned down at the corners.

"She beat you?"

"Yes. I told her there was nothing wrong with singing, and that did it. 'Spect if I'd snivelled and begged her not to shut me up she mightn't have taken the stick to me. I wasn't going to give her that satisfaction. What's a bruise or two, anyway?"

"I'd like to kill her."

Opal looked at Davey more carefully.

"You sound as though you meant that."

"I do. I hate the old faggot for what she did to you."

Suddenly the conversation had taken a personal turn and Opal wasn't sure that she liked that. Her dreams were for someone else, not for Davey. Then she dismissed her foolishness. Davey was only giving her a pat on the back.

"Well, it's over now."

"Mm, suppose so. Have you had anything to eat?"

"Not since yesterday dinner-time."

Campbell pulled a crust out of his pocket. It was none too clean, but Opal accepted it gratefully.

"Thanks, I can do with this."

"Say, Opal."

"Yes?"

"When we're both out of here, what if we were to see each other now and then?"

"Not likely, is it?"

"We could make it happen."

"Not for ages. You're to leave soon, aren't you? I shan't be free for another four years at least."

"Years pass. I'd like to see you again."

Before Opal had time to make things plain to Davey, Susie was back.

"Did you say you were going to see each other when you get out of here?" Her sadness was a thing of the past. "I think that's a splendid idea. We can all meet, can't we?"

It diffused the niggling doubt in Opal's mind and made things impersonal again.

"Yes, of course we can. You and I and Davey are bound to run into one another one day."

Campbell's smile was wry. He hadn't missed Opal's reluctance, but then she was still only a child, if a very plucky one. When she was nineteen instead of nine the situation would be different. He'd been trouble enough to her in the last twenty-four hours. This wasn't the moment to fret her any further.

"That's right, Susie," he said, his eyes still on Opal. "We've gone through too much together to be parted for good. Well, best not dance any more now, old girl. You're a spunky one; you've proved that. Now eat your bread; you deserve it."

* * *

Opal left Lockgate when she was thirteen years old. A position had been found for her as a scullery-maid in the household of a certain Mr. and Mrs. Lister.

Four months before her release she was allowed to grow her hair, and on the night before she was to set out for Southwark she was given a bath in a tin tub, scrubbed down with strong yellow soap.

Then she was fitted out with coarse underwear and a cheap dress made of black serge, handed a bag containing cap and apron and a spare pair of drawers. She was also given an admonition as to what would happen if the Listers informed the workhouse that she hadn't arrived at her destination.

How many of the threats were true Opal didn't know, but she was prepared to believe at least some of them. In any case, there really wasn't anywhere else for her to go except the streets, and that was out of the question.

Her first period had scared her more than the bodies in the morgue, for no one had warned her what happened when menstruation began. She was also acutely embarrassed by her uncleanliness and wished that her mother had explained about the monthly curse, as well as how to watch out for the bobbies.

The older women laughed at her, some with a mite of sympathy. Most of them told her in the crudest possible terms what could happen now between her and any man who fancied her. In addition to learning to read, write, dance, sing and help to steal, she had also gained a remarkable knowledge of prostitution, its rewards and its penalties.

She understood then a little more about the look in Davey Campbell's eyes just before he had left Lockgate, and it made her think about her Regent Street beau in rather a different way, too.

The Listers' house was large and rambling. The other maids grumbled constantly about the massive furniture which her ladyship insisted should be polished every day and the carpets which had to be spread with tea-leaves and then brushed until no speck of dust remained.

Opal wasn't allowed to venture above the basement. She was the lowest of the low, on her knees scrubbing from five-thirty in the morning until late at night. This activity was punctuated by the peeling of potatoes, washing pots and pans, and making tea for the senior staff.

None of the servants liked her. They had made up their minds that she was no good even before she arrived. She was a workhouse girl, and it was common knowledge that they were all lazy sluts, dirty, and prone to thieving.

When they saw her beauty their disapproval increased. No charity child ought to have hair like spun gold or eyes the colour of lapis-lazuli. They were straight eyes, too, looking through her fellow-workers as if she could read their minds. They shunned her, speaking to her only when they had to, and keeping her on the run until she was ready to drop.

But Lockgate and The Death Hole hadn't broken Opal's spirit, nor had the loss of her whole family. She had weathered those blows and had no intention of letting a gaggle of stuck-up domestics get under her skin.

Thirteen was too young to run away and seek fame and fortune. If she left the much-hated basement she would undoubtedly find herself back at Lockgate with Mrs. Crooker waiting for her with a stick.

Her greatest problem was how to keep practising her singing and dancing, a feat she'd managed in the workhouse in spite of Crooker and her fellows. At the Listers she had to share a bedroom with two other maids, given a straw pallet in one corner and told not to snore.

There was no hope of skipping about in the scullery either, and she was growing despondent when she was sent by Cook to fetch milk from the local dairy.

There was a motherly-looking woman ladling out the creamy liquid, and she gave Opal a friendly smile as the Listers' jugs were handed over.

"Not seen you before, have I? Just arrived at Mrs. Lister's?"

Opal returned the smile. For once it was nice not to have to keep one's face rigid and without expression.

"I've been there for a while, but this is the first time I've been sent on an errand. Rose usually comes, but she's left."

"Don't blame her. Rotten lot, those Listers. Mister is a pompous old fool and missus thinks she's the Empress of China. How do the others below stairs treat you?"

When Opal didn't reply the shopkeeper gave a short laugh.

"That doesn't surprise me neither. All tarred by the same brush. Where were you before you came to Southwark?"

Opal didn't hold anything back. She wasn't ashamed at having been in Lockgate, for it hadn't been her fault. She told the woman, Ivy Rogers, all about Em and the family, even confessing how they had got the money to live.

Ivy nodded, no trace of censure in her.

"Some have it hard and that's a fact. Funny your pa being a singer in a tavern. I used to do a bit of singing in a pub in Hackney when I was younger."

Opal's eyes lit up.

"You did? Oh, Mrs. Rogers, please tell me about it. Please!"

"Willingly. Nothing I like better than talking about those times; happiest days of my life."

"I want to go on the halls myself. I sing and dance, too."

"Do you, now?" Mrs. Rogers eyed Opal up and down, not wholly free of envy. The girl was exquisite, and if she really had any talent, there was nothing she couldn't do if she was prepared to work for it. "We ought to talk, you and I, but not now. If you hang about here any longer you'll be for it when you get back."

Opal's face fell.

"Yes, of course, I forgot. I must go."

"Aye, you'd best be on your way, but I've an idea."

It sounded promising, and Opal held her breath.

"If there's one thing Old Mother Lister is above all else, it's mean. Looks at every ha'penny half-a-dozen times before she spends it. What if I was to tell her I needed a strong, willing girl to help in the evenings washing out the dairy? I could say that if she'd let you come I'd give her her milk a bit cheaper."

"But why should you, for me? Of course I'd work hard for you, but – "

Ivy chuckled, her double chin shaking with mirth.

"You aren't going to work, m'dear, at least not scrubbing the floors. No, I wanted to be a real artiste once, so I know how you feel. You can practise here o'nights, and I'll help you. Know something about singing if I do say so myself."

Opal was very pale, hardly able to believe the miracle which was taking place. Then more doubts crept in.

"What if Mrs. Lister agrees to send someone but not me?"

"Then she pays full price for her milk, and I'll tell her it's gone up into the bargain."

"Do you really think you could get her to say yes?"

"Fairly sure of it. Wouldn't have mentioned it if I didn't know that tartar like I know the back of my own hand. She comes in here once a week, regular as clockwork. Wants to see if my place is clean and whether I've got any stale butter or cheese for the servants' meals. Don't you worry, lass. I did a bit of acting as well. Just you leave it to me."

Opal never found out exactly what took place between her parsimonious employer and Ivy Rogers. All she knew was that she was to be packed off at six each night to help out at the dairy, with a warning that in spite of the extra work she'd better not be late up in the mornings if she wanted to keep her position.

The first thing Mrs. Rogers did when Opal arrived was to

give her prospective pupil a good hot meal.

"You won't sing or dance on what that woman gives you," she said, setting a generous portion of stew down on the table. "Eat that up, and then we'll hear what you can do with that voice of yours."

When the plate was carefully scraped clean and a wedge of apple pie had been demolished, Ivy and Opal moved the chairs back against the wall leaving space for the performance to take place.

"When you're ready." Mrs. Rogers settled herself down by the fire, helping herself to a chocolate from the box at her elbow. "No hurry and no need to be nervous. Just pretend you're alone and you'll be fine."

Ivy listened to Opal sing, but before the latter had got through the second verse she knew what she'd found. A beautiful child with a voice like a nightingale's, whose immature young body moved with unconscious seduction as she danced.

She was silent for a long time after Opal made her curtsy. Opal could feel tears pricking behind her eyelids. Ivy hadn't liked it. It wasn't good enough for even the most modest of praise. It would mean the Listers, or somebody else like them, for the rest of her days. If Mrs. Rogers had given her efforts the thumbs down, so would the managers of the music halls.

"I'm sorry," she said at last, knowing she had to break the awkward stillness. "I'm out of practice, but I've not done much of it anyway. I've wasted your time."

Ivy selected a violet cream and turned to look at Opal.

"Wasted my time? Jesus, girl, don't you think I recognise a great gift when I hear it? You come back to-morrow night and every night after that. We'll work on you till you're perfect.

"And one day, Miss Opal Shannon, you're going to drive men mad, there's no doubt about it. Before too long you'll have the whole world at your feet, and I'll be there to see it. Come here, love, and give your new teacher a great big kiss."

Three

There was great excitement in the Grosvenor Square home of the Earl of Kynston as he and his family talked of their forthcoming visit to India.

The earl was a stocky man with a round, jolly face and twinkling brown eyes. Now and then he thought perhaps he ought to have presented a sterner father-figure to his children, but he had left it rather late in the day.

He gazed at them fondly as they sat on the rug in front of the fire laughing and talking. Handsome Edward, now eighteen, and like his beautiful mother, Charlotte. Ian and Graeme were twins, comely enough even if not possessed of the viscount's charisma. They did everything together, and, at ten years, it was almost inevitable that most of their activities were of a mischievous nature. Kynston's two daughters, Clio, fourteen, and Elspeth, sixteen, were charmers with soft, melting eyes, sweet smiles and wills like tempered steel. Stephen Adare couldn't remember when he had last won an argument with them. Their minds were agile, full of female cunning, and his heart wasn't really in his vain efforts to score a victory.

He glanced at Charlotte who sat beside the hearth, the flames flushing her face. He couldn't for the life of him understand why she had agreed to marry him. She was the daughter of a duke and could have had her pick of any nobleman around at the time Annice was contemplating matrimony for her.

Now and then he would return to the subject, asking if

she were still sure she'd made the right choice. She would laugh at him, her hazel eyes, so like Edward's, dancing with mirth.

"Yes, I'm still sure," she would reply, giving him a hug. "Goodness knows why, for you're as weak as water in disciplining the children, you've put on too much weight, you can't shoot straight, and your dancing is atrocious." Then her amusement would fade and her long fingers would caress his cheek. "You're also an idiot, Kynston. Don't you recognise a woman in love when you see one?"

The earl had been promising to take the family to India for the last two years, and now they were almost on the point of sailing. Everything was packed, the carriages ready to take them and their luggage to the docks in three days' time.

"Edward, will you fetch my shawl? I don't want to bother Maud because she's supposed to be packing my hats. She's very fractious today and keeps telling me what curries will do to my complexion. It's the cream one; you'll find it on my dressing-table stool."

For a second the viscount's hand rested in his mother's. They were very close. He was her precious first-born, she his goddess. It made a lump come into Stephen's throat to watch them together. Not every family cared so deeply for one another, and he knew how lucky he was.

Five minutes later the blow fell. Edward, not looking where he was going, went headlong down the stairs, lying in the hall, his leg under him, his face twisted in pain.

Dr. Sinclair made no bones about the situation when he had dealt with Peverell's injuries.

"His right leg is broken and it'll take some time to heal."

"But he's going to India."

Sinclair glanced at Clio and shook his head.

"Not with you, unless you can postpone your journey. He's to lie still for a while and he won't be walking for several weeks."

The Adares exchanged looks of consternation, and when Sinclair had left final instructions with the countess as to the care of her son, the family gathered in the viscount's bedroom to talk things over.

"You must go, of course." Edward was bitterly disappointed and cursing himself for his stupidity. "You can't cancel everything now."

"Well, we could – " The earl was rubbing his chin. "It'll be devilishly awkward, but we don't want to go without you."

"Sir, you'll have to. It's taken three months to get this far. I won't spoil it for you and the others."

"But, sweetheart, we can't leave you here alone." The countess was holding Edward's hand again, but more tightly this time. "I shouldn't have a minute's peace."

"Dearest, the house is awash with servants. I won't be alone."

"That's different. I'll stay with you and the others can go."

"No, no, I refuse to let you do that. Father won't go if you don't. You know that perfectly well."

They seemed to have reached an impasse when Amory, the butler, appeared to announce the arrival of the Dowager Duchess of Ware.

"Annice?" The earl looked blank. "What on earth is she doing here? She can't stand London."

Amory coughed discreetly.

"I didn't ask her, m'lord. Didn't think it was my place."

"No, you're right. You'd only have got your head bitten off if you'd tried." Stephen looked helplessly at his wife. "All right, we'll come down."

"No need." Annice was puffed from mounting the stairs, but as mettlesome as ever. "Really, Peverell, how could you be so clumsy? Whatever are you going to do at Court if you keep tripping over your own feet?"

"Annice! Oh, I'm so glad to see you." Edward tried to move, and turned whiter still. "Do come and tell mother and father that they must go to India. They want to stay with me, but it's absurd."

"Of course it is. Whoever would want to stay with you when they could see the Taj Mahal?"

"You'll come and live here for a while, won't you, just until they get home again?"

The earl and countess began immediate protestations, the former running over the steps necessary to bring their holiday plans to an end. Her Grace was impatient.

"Stephen, for goodness sake stop muttering. Naturally you must go. You can't disappoint the children. If Edward has had to take to his bed he's got no one but himself to thank for it."

"Mother, can you really manage?" Charlotte was still anxious. "Why are you in town anyway?"

"I'm here because I've had to visit a sick friend. Now I've got another invalid dumped on me. As to managing! Do you imagine I'm senile? I can cope with this numskull and a dozen more like him. Don't cluck over him as if he were a day-old chick. He's a man, though sometimes I wonder – "

"You see?" Edward was quick to support the duchess. "I'll be all right. Don't take any notice of Annie, she's always like that."

"Yes, dear, I know. She's my mother."

"But you're afraid of her and I'm not. Father, say you'll go this very minute or I shall try to get out of bed."

"If you do you'll get a box round your ears, my lad." Annice was removing her hat-pins, casting a fierce look at the viscount. "And I'm glad to know that your mother shews some respect for me, which is more than you do. Now, Stephen – "

"I suppose it'll be all right." Kynston was distracted, still unhappy about leaving his heir behind. "It's good of you, Annice, but – "

"But nothing. Go away, all of you. I'm in charge of the sick-room now and I intend to start as I mean to go on. Charlotte, bring me back some of those lovely gold earrings. You know, the sort that tinkle and jangle when you walk."

When Edward and Annice were at last alone, the duchess said quietly:

"I'm sorry, m'dear. Bad luck for you."

Edward shrugged, putting a brave face on things.

"It is rather, but, as you said, it was my own fault. I do hope you're not going to take advantage of my weakened position to bully me."

"Certainly I am. I'd be a fool not to. Now I'm going to see the servants and give them my orders."

"Poor devils. You won't forget my dinner, will you?"

"Bread and milk."

Their eyes met again, and both smiled. Then the viscount lay back against the pillows and, not for the first time since that Christmas Eve in Regent Street, began to think about the girl in the shabby blue dress.

* * *

Under Mrs. Rogers' guidance, Opal's singing and dancing improved by leaps and bounds. Ivy knew many of the current songs and exactly how they should be put over. She had found a couple of old silk dresses which she had worn in her tavern days, cutting them up and altering them so that Opal could have full skirts to swish as she glided and spun round the floor.

She was happier than she'd been since before the night of the fire. She couldn't put all of the sadness behind her, and she still had some nightmares, but now she had something really worth while to work for.

The servants at the Listers looked at her with renewed hostility. They saw the glowing colour in her cheeks, the rounding of her limbs and swelling breasts, the sparkle in her eyes.

" 'Ope you've not got yourself tied up with some boy," said Cook as she handed Opal a large basket of carrots to deal with. "You're only thirteen and far too young for that sort of thing."

"There's no boy." Opal stopped thinking about Ivy and the music halls. She had let her mask slip and shewn her new contentment. Now she had to repair the damage, her face growing blank again. "Nothing like that, Mrs. Shoesmith."

"I 'opes not. Missus wouldn't like it. You'd get packed off back to Lockgate, and that mightn't be such a bad thing; come to think of it. Not used to your kind 'ere. None of us felt it were fair to 'ave you foisted on us."

"There is no boy." Opal repeated the words stonily. "I'm sorry you don't like me, but I couldn't help being in the workhouse. My father and two brothers died in a fire. My mother got pneumonia and then she died, too."

"You didn't tell us that before."

"I didn't think you'd be interested."

Prosser and Maples, two of the maids, stopped their work and looked at Opal as if they were seeing her for the first time. Prosser was about to say something sympathetic, but envy stifled her good intentions at birth. Shannon had everything which she, Prosser, longed for. Thick, sun-coloured hair instead of mouse-brown; large blue eyes instead of small black ones; a mouth of deepest pink, beautifully fashioned, instead of thin, pinched lips which turned down at the corners.

"Very 'ard for you, I'm sure." Cook had no charitable thoughts whatsoever. She was just irritated because Opal hadn't revealed her whole history at an earlier stage. "Still, what I says goes. I'll be keepin' an eye on you, and if I don't like what I sees it'll be straight to the mistress I'll be goin'."

"It's not that I mind them hating me," said Opal to Mrs. Rogers that night. "I don't care tuppence what they think. What I'm afraid of is that Mrs. Shoesmith may tell Mrs. Lister lies about me and I'll find myself back at Lockgate."

Ivy opened a new box of chocolates, and it made Opal think of her mother. Em had had a penchant for sweets, not that she'd got them very often. But a mouthful of chocolate or a piece of candy had never failed to put her in a good mood.

"That won't happen."

"It might. They're not very nice people, Cook and the others. They resent me because I was a pauper."

Ivy cackled.

"They resent you 'cos you're as pretty as a picture and they're not. I've seen 'em, don't forget. Prosser, Maples, Chorley and that girl who waits on Madam Lister. And stop worrying. If that old besom doesn't want you any more I'll take you on full-time in the dairy. You won't go back to the workhouse whatever happens."

Opal went to kneel beside Ivy and held the latter's hand against her cheek.

"You are so kind to me," she said, and her voice wasn't steady. "Goodness knows what I'd be like if you weren't my friend."

"Stuff and nonsense! You'd still be an eyeful and you'd still be able to sing and dance."

"Not in Mrs. Lister's kitchen."

"No, maybe not. Here, stop that grizzling. I've got a new song for you to learn. Laura Bell sings it at *The Canterbury Hall*, and I'm told it's Charles Morton's favourite. He's a great man in the world you want to enter, so you'd best get to know the words pretty damn quick."

"All right, if you say so. Ivy, do you think I'll ever meet Mr. Morton? I'd like to because I've heard so much about him."

"Where you're going you won't be able to avoid him. Now, you can have just one chocolate. Too many and you'd get fat like me. And no more tears, mind."

"I was only crying because I love you."

Ivy's own eyes were moist as she hugged Opal to her.

"I know, chicken, I know. Still, I'm just as lucky as you. Never had children, but I'd always wanted a daughter to keep me company, and now I've got one. I've got you, Opal Shannon, and you're stuck with me for good."

* * *

While Opal and Mrs. Rogers were exchanging embraces, Davey Campbell, a mature eighteen-year-old, was looking out of his bedroom window, reviewing the last four years of his life.

The workhouse had given him a smattering of knowledge about shoemaking, and a position had been found for him with one Herbert Walsh. Herbert and the Workhouse Master could have been peas from the same pod, and after forty-eight hours Davey had run away. He had no intention of adopting Walsh's trade, nor tolerating the vicious temper of his new employer.

He had lived rough for two weeks, stealing food when he could, going hungry when he couldn't. He had slept in empty, derelict properties, ignoring warning signs as to their dangerous state, kicking rats out of the way when they became too troublesome.

Then he had seen the old man. He was seventy, if he'd been a day. A frail creature, poorly clad, and struggling with a barrow far too heavy for him. It was clear that he'd been trying to sell vegetables and fruit, but, judging by the load he was taking home, he hadn't had much success.

It was the opportunity which Davey had been waiting for; he had felt it in his bones as he approached the vendor.

He hadn't wasted time with preliminaries. It had been raining all day and he and the old man were soaked to the skin. Idle conversation would have been out of place.

"If I help you, will you lend me your barrow?"

The man, whose name had turned out to be Phineas Weech, had eyed Davey with suspicion. He ached all over and wished with all his heart that he had had something better to go back to than one lonely room in a slum. He was in no mood for pesky youths and said so uncompromisingly.

"I mean it." Campbell had stood his ground, not at all put off by Weech's reaction. It was just what he'd expected. "I'll push your barrow for you if you'll let me use it for a while to-morrow."

"What you got to sell, eh?"

"I don't know yet. Depends what I can pick up."

"Thievin', you mean?" Weech had shaken his head. "Don't do it, boy, it ain't worth it."

"I'll take the risk."

Weech had grunted. He liked the look of Davey's square chin and direct grey eyes. Something about the lad reminded him of Harry, his dead son, but he hadn't agreed at once.

"I don't want no part of pinching stuff."

"You won't be asked to. If I get caught, I shan't say where I got the barrow."

After a few more moments of hesitation Weech had said: "Tell you what. I've had the screws real bad these last few days. You take the barrow out to-morrow and sell me stuff. I'll pay you a quarter of what you take and then you can save and buy some goods of your own, honest-like."

Campbell had given an inward sigh of relief.

It was a small enough proposition, but it had been a start.

"I accept."

"Where are you livin'?"

"Nowhere."

"Must live somewhere."

"In the streets or any old building I can find. Doesn't matter; I'm strong."

" 'Ow old are you?"

"Fourteen, going on fifteen."

Weech had given another grunt.

"Best come 'ome with me. Ain't nothin' much, but it keeps the rain out. Can only give you tea and bread and cheese."

To Davey, who had had nothing to eat for two days, it had sounded like a king's banquet, and from that moment on he had never looked back.

He had a flair for salesmanship, getting rid of even the limpest of lettuces and cabbages. The barrow was always empty by five in the afternoon, and then he began to deal with his own stuff. He had learned to pick things up cheaply and sell at a profit. His smile had wooed the female customers, and his sharp wits and sense of humour brought approval from his fellow costermongers.

When Weech died two years later no one claimed his room, his personal possessions, such as they were, or his barrow. Davey had found a small box with some sovereigns in it and had used a few of them to take a stall in the market.

At seventeen he had decided to acquire his first shop. He had had enough experience by then to know what buying and selling were all about. He wanted more than a barrow or a stall, for there were still many rungs of the ladder to climb.

He had had his eye on a small corner shop for some time. It belonged to an elderly widow, and its windows had been grimy, the paintwork on the door and shutters peeled away. Inside, it was even worse, but Davey had seen at once how it could look when a bit of elbow-grease had been applied.

At first, the widow had flatly refused to sell. Then, when she had seen how keen Campbell was, she named her price, insisting that she should have sixpence from every pound he took into the bargain. Age might have withered her, but she was as tough as Davey when it came to discussing money.

Davey had knocked down the initial demand to a more realistic figure, not worrying about the sixpences. He didn't think she'd last all that long and it would probably be the same for her when she died as it had been for Weech. Even if a relative did appear on the scene they wouldn't be difficult to deal with. He would tell them it had been an outright sale and none could prove otherwise.

The widow had sold a miscellany of goods, but none which those living round about were likely to want. Davey had closed the place for four days, scrubbing, washing, painting and polishing. Then he had used the rest of his savings to stock the shelves with the basic necessities of life, plus useful things like string, boot-laces, reels of cotton, candles, bundles of firewood and soap.

Word had spread quickly of the excellent quality of young Mr. Campbell's bread, tea-cakes and butter. His cheese, the housewives had told one another, was the best they'd ever tasted, and soon he had had to hire a boy to help with deliveries of larger orders.

The widow had collected quite a few sixpences before she fell ill and was taken to the infirmary, where she had died within the week.

Davey stirred, pulling the curtain aside so that he could watch the people passing by, most of whom were his customers. He was ready to buy his second shop now, and still had the market stall which was flourishing.

He lived above the shop, making himself comfortable but not wasting good brass on luxuries. He had made a number of friends with whom he supped a pint in the local pub. He had also found that he was attractive to women of a certain sort and wasn't short of company when he felt in the mood for a spot of love-making.

He often thought about Susie Phelps and even more about Opal and her fortitude. Once, after he'd established himself, he had gone back to Lockgate to ask if he could see Opal. The matron had informed him frostily that Shannon had been found a position but flatly refused to give him the address.

He poured himself a beer, wondering if he really would see the girls again. It had been easy enough when they were all in the House together to say that they'd meet when they were older. Now they'd gone their separate ways it seemed less likely.

Then he frowned. He hadn't got as far as he had without unwavering determination. He could spare a little of that strength of purpose to find out where Opal was. After the second shop was on its feet he'd have another try.

"I won't give up that easily," he said under his breath. "I'll find you, girl."

The young woman gracing his bed rolled over as he spoke.

"What's that, Davey? Didn't 'ear you."

"You weren't meant to."

He turned to look at her, plump, naked and waiting for him to finish his drink. She wasn't bad to look at, even if she was a prostitute, and she satisfied him well enough.

"Secrets?" She stretched like a contented cat. It wasn't only Campbell's money which interested her. He was an exciting lover, fierce as a tiger, as she told her friends when they met over a glass of gin. "Tell us about 'em."

"If I did, they wouldn't be secrets any more, would they?"

"I bet they're about another woman."

He saw her chagrin as he began to undress.

"None of your business if they are."

"I thought you loved me."

He gave a caustic laugh.

"No you didn't. Love doesn't come in to what we do up here together."

She looked sulkier still.

"Not sure I like it when you talk that way."

"Then you'll have to lump it, won't you?" His arms were round her, hard and demanding, Opal forgotten for the moment. "Come here, you luscious bitch and stop your bloody nonsense. It's about time you started earning what I pay you for, so shut up and give me a kiss."

* * *

"Not all of them, Annie! No, it can't be true."

"I'm afraid it is, my dear."

"I don't believe it."

Her Grace sat up very straight, the task before her the most difficult one she'd ever have to tackle. Her own pain was almost past bearing, but her grandson needed her comfort and her strength and she wasn't going to fail him.

"You'll have to accept it, dreadful though it is. They were five days out of port when it happened. I don't know all the facts, but the ship went down quickly, I'm told. There were very few survivors. Some sort of explosion in the engine-room, probably. We shall get more details later."

"But they were on their way home. Mother, father and – "

"Yes they were. My dearest Charlotte and her babies."

Edward's face was bleached as he looked down at his grandmother.

"I'm sorry; it's quite as ghastly for you. It's just that it doesn't seem real. It's like a bad dream, and I'm sure I'm going to wake up in a minute and find that everything's as it was before."

"I wish it were a nightmare. In a way it is, but we shan't awaken from it. It will be with us until we go to our graves."

"They won't have graves, will they?"

The duchess cursed her careless choice of words.

"Yes they will. The oceans of the world have always been burial grounds. Oh, my dear, my dear, thank God you didn't go, too."

"I wish I had." Edward was in agony. "I'd rather have gone down with them. It would have been better than never seeing any of them again."

"You'll see them all again one day."

"In heaven? Don't talk to me of heaven or of God either, not now. How can there be a God? Or, if there is one, how could He let this happen?"

"You'll have to find your own answer to that. Meanwhile, we have to be practical."

"How can I be practical when I've lost everyone I love?"

"Have you no shred of feeling left for me?"

"Yes, of course I have. I'm sorry, I didn't mean – "

"I know what you meant and there's no need for an apology. I'm raging inside, just as you are. Part of me is screaming at the gross unfairness of it all. Another part is dying of the hurt in me."

Edward knelt by her side, putting an arm round her.

"None of that shews. How can you be so controlled?"

"Because I was brought up that way. In any event, I've got

you to think about now. I shall live here in Grosvenor Square in future. You must go back to Cambridge, and when you come down you'll have to take your place in society as your mother and father would have wanted you to do. You're the Earl of Kynston now and you've a great fortune to manage, along with the Wiltshire and Devonshire estates. I know this isn't the ideal time or place for real plans, but one day you'll have to marry. You must have an heir."

"How can you even think of such things at a time like this?"

"I know it seems heartless to talk of marriage and children when you're grieving so, but don't you see how important they are? Who would have thought three months ago that you would be the only Adare alive today?"

"But – "

"No, m'dear, I'm not going to mince matters nor baby you. You're a man and you've got to accept your responsibilities, however tragically they've been forced upon you. I'm old, but I'm not done for yet, and I'll help you all I can. But in the end only you can keep the family name alive."

Edward was silent for a long while. Then he said quietly:

"You're right, of course, as you always are. I won't make you ashamed of me. I promise."

"I know that. I could never be anything but proud of you."

"Don't be too kind; you'll make me cry."

"Tears are acceptable in private."

"I'm glad because I don't think I'm going to be able to hold mine back for much longer. Oh, Annie, Annie, why were they taken from us like this? Dear Christ! Why did they all have to die?"

Four

On her fifteenth birthday, Opal received from Ivy Rogers a gift which was to change her life.

It was a small silk purse, delicately embroidered, with a fine ribbon attached to it so that one could wear it round the neck. It contained five sovereigns, and at first Opal had protested that she couldn't take so much from Ivy.

"You've taught me everything I know. That's present enough."

"I only polished up what you'd already got." Ivy had patted her pupil's cheek. " 'Sides, I don't want you to look on this as just money. It's to be more than that."

"How?"

"It's freedom. If at any time I had to go away, or anything happened to me and you couldn't stand those perishing Listers any more, you could keep yourself till you got another place."

"Yes, I see." Something cold had touched Opal's heart. "You're not going away, are you?"

"Not expecting to, not for a while anyway."

"And what could happen to you?"

"Don't suppose anything will. Best to be on the safe side, just in case."

Ivy had refused to discuss the matter any further, extracting a promise from Opal that the latter would always wear her purse hidden under her shift, so that no one knew she had it and thus couldn't steal it from her.

Two weeks later when Ivy was in the middle of a raucous

song, she clutched at her chest, choking on the words as she slumped to the floor. By the time the horrified Opal had called for help from a neighbour, and a doctor had been found, Ivy Rogers was dead.

Opal remembered the evening of her birthday, and as the doctor was leaving she ventured a question.

"Did she know she was going to die?"

Dr. Parnell glanced down at the white-faced girl and nodded.

"Yes, she knew. I told her a week or two ago that heart of hers wouldn't last long. I also told her she ought to rest, but she wouldn't listen to me. Pig-headed, of course, but a game old bird. Friend of yours, was she?"

"The best I ever had."

"I'm sorry. It's always hard to lose friends."

After that, life at the Listers grew more and more intolerable, until one morning after Mrs. Lister had been particularly vixenish Opal ran away. She packed what few possessions she had in a paper bag, understanding then why Ivy had insisted on her accepting the sovereigns. She wouldn't starve while she looked for another job. She thought about what the doctor had said and agreed with him. Mrs. Rogers had indeed been a game old bird. She had kept her mortal illness to herself and had given her pupil nothing but love and encouragement right up to the last.

Opal hadn't the faintest idea how to go about finding another post, for she hadn't had to face such a situation before. One couldn't just knock on people's doors and ask if they wanted help in their sculleries. Going back to Lockgate was out of the question, but she remembered the nervous young curate who had visited the workhouse twice a week. She knew where his church was and had a vague idea to call there to see if he had any ideas. Even if he had left the parish there might be another cleric willing to make a suggestion and not report her departure from the Listers to the Workhouse Master.

Then she decided that she would see something of

London before calling at St. Mary's. She walked for a long time and by mid-afternoon found herself in Grosvenor Square surrounded by palatial mansions. She stopped outside one, admiring its graceful pillars and the way its brass knocker shone. The house made her think of the boy in Regent Street, who had never really left her mind. Often days had gone by when she was too busy to think of him. Then something would happen to remind her of that moment when he had smiled at her and she would find that she was covered in goose-pimples.

She hoped he did live in comfort; she liked to think of him moving in a world of such luxury. She was so busy with her thoughts that she didn't notice the man walking towards her.

The last two years had been hard for Edward Adare, now nearing his majority. For the first few months after his family had been lost at sea he could think of nothing else. He kept picturing them, one by one, wondering what they had felt when they knew the ship was sinking.

The girls would probably have wept and clung to their father; even the fearless twins might have cried out in dread. He knew that Charlotte would have been brave. She would have held the children to her, soothing them and telling them that everything was going to be all right, but of course it hadn't been. His adored mother had drowned along with the others.

Annice had been like a rock. He knew that she suffered every bit as much as he did, but she had shewn no sign of it after the awful day when she had to break the news to him. She had supported him with love, terse with him if she thought he had been weakening or becoming too morbid. She had mustered every ounce of strength to get him through the ordeal, which at one point he thought would never end.

Then one day, quite unexpectedly, he was able to face what had happened without the dreadful grief clawing him inside like a wild beast. As the weeks went by the torment grew less and less painful. He never forgot them, not for a minute, but he had come to terms with the tragedy and at last found that he could remember them without wanting to weep.

As he approached his home he noticed the girl and his heart missed a beat. It had been six years since that happy Christmas Eve, but he recognised her at once. She had turned her head, suddenly aware of his presence, and her blue eyes were looking into his exactly as they had done on the day they had first met.

Opal's pulse was racing. She had reconciled herself to the fact that she would never have more than a memory of her secret love, but there he was in flesh and blood, smiling at her as he had done once before.

Edward raised his hat, bidding her good-afternoon. He was glad there was colour in her cheeks this time and that her lips weren't bloodless. She was still slender, but the bones no longer shewed beneath the skin. The years had turned a pretty child into a delightful girl, and he felt another kind of sadness assail him.

He had hoped so much that he would see her again, but his wish was tainted by the knowledge that nothing could come of such a meeting. They were trapped in their respective cages from which they could never escape.

Opal was searching Edward's face just as avidly. He had grown even more handsome and was so debonair. She was ashamed of her old black serge and shawl, for he must have thought her a dreadful dowd in them.

Edward broke the spell. He didn't want her to run away this time. He had to talk to her and find out her name, even if this was the last time they would encounter each other. He had a new picture of her to treasure in his mind, but he wanted words as well.

"I'm Edward Adare," he said, and held out his hand. "Tell me your name."

"It's Opal, sir; Opal Shannon."

"Opal suits you. Why are you waiting outside my house?"

She wasn't overawed by him. She had always been able to speak up for herself, and Ivy Rogers had given her even more self-confidence.

"I didn't know it was yours, but I'm glad it is. It looks so fine. I just stopped to admire it, that's all."

"What are you doing in this part of London? Do you work near here?"

"No, I'd like to, but I don't suppose anyone would take me on. You see, I ran away from my job in Southwark this morning. I couldn't stand Mrs. Lister a second longer, and as Ivy had given me – " She stopped abruptly. "I'm sorry, I didn't mean to bore you."

"You weren't boring me. Do go on. I already dislike Mrs. Lister most heartily, and who is Ivy?"

"Was – she's dead. It's sad to lose someone you love, isn't it?"

Opal saw the pain in Adare's eyes and could have kicked herself. Obviously he, too, had suffered a bereavement, and she had killed the laughter in him by mentioning death.

"Yes it is." Edward pushed his family gently aside, knowing they would understand about the few precious minutes he was stealing.

"What did Ivy give you? Tell me all about it."

"Do you really want to hear? All of it?"

"Every last detail."

When she had related her story and how Ivy had been helping her to realise a great ambition, he said musingly:

"Well, I can't do anything about the music halls, but as you're looking for a post as a kitchen-maid you might as well try here. I heard my grandmother say we needed another one. Before I shew you where the servants' entrance is, tell me what sort of songs you're going to sing if you manage to get on the halls."

Opal's chin was stubborn.

"I'll get there, don't worry about that. I'll sing something for you now if you like."

"There's nothing I'd enjoy more."

When Opal began a somewhat risqué number, marvellously graceful even in clumpy boots and frayed skirt, Edward's smile faded. She was very young, but he knew he wanted her. He would always want her, no matter what the pattern of his life was to be. He longed to watch her grow up and to make her his when the time was ripe, but it was hopeless.

It wasn't until she made her curtsy to him that they realised she had attracted a small crowd, now shewing their whole-hearted approval of her performance.

"Oh dear." Edward took her arm quickly and hastened her round the corner. "I didn't think what I was doing. I hope you're not embarrassed."

She laughed, and he felt as if he were intoxicated.

"Because people liked me? No, I won't be satisfied until they stand up in their seats and cheer me. Still, that won't be for a while yet. Is there really a vacancy here?"

"Yes. Ring that bell and ask for Mrs. Palmer. She's the housekeeper. I think I'd better make good my escape. You don't think I'm deserting you, do you? It's simply that – "

"No, I know you've got to go."

"If you do get the position – "

For a moment they were the only two in the world, reading each other's thoughts.

"We won't be seeing each other again," said Opal finally. "You'll be upstairs and I'll be down. It's all right. I'll go on remembering you whatever Mrs. Palmer decides."

"Nor will I forget you. I'll think of you every day."

It was Whicker who informed the duchess that a girl had been singing and dancing on the pavement outside.

"It wasn't at all a nice song, Your Grace; quite vulgar in fact. Master Edward was clapping, though, just like the others."

Annice frowned.

"What others?"

"Passers-by who stopped to watch her. She's gone round to the servants' entrance."

"Oh has she? Go down and tell Mrs. Palmer I want to see this wench."

"Yes, Your Grace, but surely you wouldn't take her on? Not suitable at all, I wouldn't have thought, although it's the first time I've heard Master Edward laugh since – "

Annice's scowl had deepened.

"For heaven's sake stop calling him Master Edward. He's not five years old. And go and do as I say or Mrs. Palmer may send her packing before I get the chance to talk to her."

When Opal was shewn into the drawing-room she looked about her in astonishment. She had never seen such a room before and was completely overawed. So many oil-paintings in gilt frames on the pale blue walls; rich silk drapes at the tall windows; a thick carpet into which one's feet sank; ornaments of silver, gold and crystal, and furniture covered with heavy brocade.

Then she looked at the duchess and gave a polite bob.

"You wanted to see me, m'am?"

Annice had taken stock of Opal during that brief pause, not missing so much as a stitch in the shabby dress. The duchess was used to lovely females in her world, but the girl whom Edward had applauded put the lot of them in the shade. Another nerve twitched inside Annice as she said calmly:

"You should address me as Your Grace, and yes, I did want to see you. What do you mean by prancing about outside my front door?"

If she had expected Opal to hang her head or shuffle nervously she was disappointed. Her unexpected visitor met her piercing gaze with composure.

"I wasn't prancing, Your Grace. I was singing and dancing."

"Comes to the same thing."

"Not the way I do it."

The duchess had always liked a woman with spirit, but she forced herself to look more severe than ever because this one was dangerous.

"Really, and watch your tongue when you speak to me. What's this I hear about you applying for a position as a kitchen-maid?"

"I have to find a job somehow and that's what I was until this morning. Then I ran away."

"Did you, indeed? Left your mistress in the lurch, I suppose?"

"I think Mrs. Lister was probably glad to see me go."

"Mm, no doubt she was, come to think of it. Where were you before that?"

The duchess saw Opal straighten her shoulders and take a deep breath, wondering what was coming next.

"I was in the workhouse."

"I see."

"I don't suppose you do, Your Grace, but it doesn't really matter. You're not going to take me on, are you?"

Annice's approval increased, but the risk was still there. The combination of such beauty and a strong will would be irresistible to any man. Whicker had said that Edward was laughing for the first time since the family drowned and that made it all the more imperative to get rid of Miss Shannon as quickly as possible.

"I'm told you danced for my grandson."

"Yes, for Mr. Adare."

"Is that what he told you his name was?"

Opal was taken aback.

"Yes, Edward Adare. Why, isn't it his real name?"

"It's his name, but it's his title which matters. He's the Earl of Kynston and he should have told you so."

"An earl?" Opal felt shock run through her. It seemed to put Edward further away than ever. "I didn't know."

"Of course you didn't, how could you? Miss Shannon, sometimes susceptible young men get fanciful notions into their heads. They're not mature enough to make sound judgments."

"About someone like me?"

"Exactly."

Annice found herself warming yet again to Opal in spite of her fears about the girl. She was sharp-witted as well as a delight to the eye.

"I knew I'd never mean anything to him, but I've thought a lot about him since we first met. I couldn't help it."

The duchess sat up at that.

"You've met before? How? When?"

"In Regent Street, a long time ago."

"I think you'd better tell me all about it, don't you. Are you hungry?"

"Famished."

Opal's smile dazzled Annice; it would dazzle Edward, too. Hastily, Her Grace rang for a footman and demanded that food and hot chocolate be brought to the drawing-room at once.

When Opal had finished her meal and her tale, Annice nodded.

"You're an honest little creature. Not many would have admitted all that you have just confessed. I'm sorry about your family. I, too, know what it's like to lose loved ones."

Opal saw the same look on the duchess's face as she'd seen on the earl's, but she didn't ask questions. Whatever common loss Edward and his grandmother shared, neither wanted to talk about it.

"Shall I go now? It was kind of you to give me the food."

"You're welcome to it, and wait a moment. I've had an idea."

"Of someone who might want a kitchen-maid?"

"You don't want to go into service, do you? You want to be a music hall artiste."

"Yes, but that won't happen for ages. I'm too young."

"True, but if you worked in a tavern where there was singing and dancing and other entertainments it might lead to something in the end."

Opal's eyes were shining, and Her Grace shook her head. Sometimes God did such inexplicable things. For no apparent reason He had taken Charlotte and the others long before their natural span and had given a pauper child an exquisite beauty which belonged in a king's palace. But it wasn't her place to question the Almighty, and she smiled.

"We had a parlour-maid here some years ago. Her name was Alice Dabbs. She married a man who ran a tavern in Whitechapel, and she told me all about the goings-on there. I understand such places were the beginning of these new-fangled music halls."

"Yes, those and the song and supper-rooms. Pa told me that."

"Well, there you are. I'll give you a letter of introduction to Alice. I believe her husband's been dead for quite a while, but she runs his place very efficiently, so I hear."

"Do you really think she'd have me?"

"Yes, if I ask her to."

"You'd do that for me?"

Her Grace gave Opal a very straight look.

"I am doing it for my grandson. Do I make myself clear, Miss Shannon?"

It was Opal's turn to smile, but sadly.

"Yes, but you didn't need to bribe me. I'd never do anything to hurt him. I'm fifteen, poor, and come from a family who made their living picking pockets. He's only a dream person to me."

"It's what you are to him which concerns me." The duchess was blunt. "The further away you are from Grosvenor Square the easier I shall sleep at night. Whitechapel is a good way off. But there is another reason why I'm going to write to Alice."

"Yes, Your Grace?"

"I'm a fool, I suppose, but I'd like to help you. You've had a hard life and an unhappy one. Perhaps at Alice's you'll find your luck changes."

"I hope so and I do truly thank you."

"It's nothing, and, my dear –"

"Yes?"

"Stop dreaming." Annice was very gentle, remembering how she had felt when she was young and had fallen in love with a man whom her parents deemed unsuitable. She could still recall how much it had hurt when she'd been sent to France to finish her education. "We've only got a short time on this earth so we ought to make the most of it. When you're older, find a decent man who'll treat you well, and marry him. Have babies and cherish them, for they're your future. Forget Kynston."

"I'll never be able to do that; I'd be lying if I said I could. I couldn't tell you a fib, not after what you're doing for me, but I won't see your grandson again."

When the duchess reached her writing-desk she turned and looked back at Opal.

"I hope in time you will forget him for your own sake. You're a nice child and I don't want you to suffer more than you've done already. The only thing Edward Adare can do for you is to break your heart and I wouldn't like that to happen. No, I wouldn't like that at all."

* * *

Fortified by the duchess's sustaining meal, Opal decided to walk to Whitechapel.

She had a few coppers in her pocket and her precious sovereigns were still untouched. She decided to buy herself a few more clothes before she reached *Barney's Ale House,* the establishment run by Alice Dabbs. The place to find the cheapest garments would be in a market. She hadn't money to waste on the grand shops she passed on her way out of central London.

When she reached Whitechapel she found what she was looking for. It was late in the afternoon by then and the sky was darkening. The air was filled with smuts, dust, soot and ribald voices, but Opal was used to that. It wasn't so very different from Seven Dials where she and Em used to do the marketing, one way or another.

She had to hop out of the way of horse-traffic, rumbling over cobblestones, dodging the mud and filth of the streets.

Beggars whined at her; women lurched out of gin palaces and bumped into her. She managed to avoid bodily harm as she reached the long row of stalls, pitches, barrows and baskets laden with every commodity imaginable.

Leaving the temptation of artificial flowers, fancy combs, umbrellas, looking-glasses and ribbons, Opal made for a trader selling modest gowns and other apparel.

She chose two dresses, one a sturdy blue print, the other made of black alpaca, a warm shawl and some underwear. It came to rather a lot, but the red-cheeked woman who served her knocked a bit off because, as she said, Opal reminded her of her daughter.

On to the next pitch for hosiery and handkerchiefs, and further on still to buy some lighter-weight boots. The boot-man was friendly, too. Seeing how laden Opal was he found a clean sack in which she could carry away her goods.

She asked the vendor the way to *Barney's Ale House*, listening carefully to his instructions, but as she began the last lap of her journey she came upon something which made her forget all about her destination.

What had once been a shop with a room behind it had been converted into a penny gaff. The front wall had been removed so it was open to the street, the parlour similarly thrown into the shop to make one largish space for the audience.

Opal couldn't resist the temptation. She vowed she wouldn't stay long, for she knew she ought to be making for the safety of Mrs. Dabbs' public house. She paid her penny and somehow squeezed herself in with all the other people crammed together.

The noise was deafening, the air heavy with cheap tobacco, gin, sweat, and fried fish, but she wasn't put off by such minor things. At one end was a crude stage made from planks fastened to trestles, with a pierced gas-pipe running in front of it to provide footlights.

There were stuffed animal heads on the grimy walls and the oddest pictures upon which Opal didn't dwell. Instead, she wriggled to the front of the mob, rubbing shoulders with costermongers, painted ladies of the night, tramps and other shady-looking men who clearly followed the same profession as her mother had done.

At last the babble died down and gas-lights in the main room were lowered. From the wings, hidden by torn curtains, three characters emerged. Their costumes and make-up were bizarre, but Opal and the rest had no quarrel with that. The comedy had started, and everyone settled down to enjoy themselves and to call out abuse, or raise a cheer, depending on the skill of the actors.

Half an hour later Opal emerged, still bemused. At last she had seen a penny gaff, and although it wasn't what she wanted for herself it was an experience she knew she would never forget.

Barney's Ale House proved to be a good-sized tavern, with a main room for beer drinkers and a separate free-and-easy, where men closeted themselves to sing glees and other popular songs.

It was plainly furnished, but spotlessly clean, and Opal felt her spirits rise. She was afraid Mrs. Dabbs' place might turn out to be as dirty as the gaff. Then she realised how foolish her doubts had been. The duchess would never have sent her to Alice if the latter's public house was unsuitable.

Alice Dabbs was small, thin and very chic in a gown of violet taffeta with pagoda sleeves and a full skirt trimmed with broad bands of ribbon. She read the letter handed to her and then gave Opal a good looking over.

"Fancy that. Never thought I'd hear from Her Grace again. Decent sort, she is, in spite of her sharp tongue. Well, Miss Opal Shannon, you must have made a good impression on her."

Opal started as she meant to go on, with stark honesty.

"She wanted me out of the way because of the earl."

"Master Edward? How does he come into this?"

"It's rather difficult to explain and I don't suppose the

duchess mentions how my mother made her living, does she?"

Alice's shrewd black eyes swept over Opal again, her assessment quite as detailed as the duchess's had been.

"No, she doesn't."

"I ought to tell you. Wouldn't be right if I didn't, seeing that Her Grace is asking you to give me a job."

"All right, you'd better come into the parlour. Jed, look after things for me, will you? I've someone to see, private like."

"Well, whatever else you are, or aren't, you're honest," said Alice when Opal had finished baring her soul. "You told the duchess all this, too?"

"Of course; I had to. She said I was honest as well, but you do understand why she didn't want me as a kitchen-maid?"

"Only too well. I'd have got rid of you, too, if I'd been in her place."

Opal was sad.

"I'm sorry I won't see the earl again. In a way it would have been better if I'd never met him in the first instance, wouldn't it?"

"Much, but you can't turn the clock back. Just you forget all about him, my girl. No use crying for the moon. Now, what can you do?"

"Sing and dance."

"You'll have to do a good deal more than that here." Mrs. Dabbs folded the duchess's note and put it away. "Those who entertain here at night have to help scrub floors and tables, peel potatoes, fetch and carry, and clean the brasses. We all muck in, for this isn't *The Canterbury Hall.*"

"Of course, I'll do anything. I know all about scrubbing and peeling vegetables. Goodness knows I did enough of that sort of thing at the Listers'. Mrs. Dabbs."

"Yes?"

"You mentioned *The Canterbury Hall*. I've heard a lot about it but I've never seen it. Do you know it?"

"Yes, been there plenty of times. Very grand, and that Mr. Morton's a real nice gent."

"Will you tell me about it?"

"Maybe, if I've got a minute to spare, which isn't likely. Run off my feet morning and night keeping this place up to scratch. Now, let's hear you sing. Don't want my customers frightened away if you've got a voice like a corncrake."

When Opal had finished a gay little song and done a few dance steps to accompany it, Mrs. Dabbs was as quiet as Ivy Rogers had been when the latter had first heard Opal sing.

"Was it all right? Do you think your customers will run away?"

Alice shook her head, her meditation over.

"Not if they've got any sense. You're a smasher and no mistake. You belong on a proper stage."

"I'll be on one when I'm older. Meantime, will you take me on? I won't need much to eat and I'll work my fingers to the bone for you."

Alice laughed, and Opal's tension left her. It was going to be fine; Alice liked her, she could tell.

"I'll feed you properly, don't fret about that. As to work, I'll only expect you to do your fair share, no more no less. And you can entertain the men of an evening. They'll go for you, or I'll eat my best Sunday bonnet. Now, you'd better come and meet the rest of the staff. Be nice to the pot-men and those who drink here, but don't let them take liberties. If they say or do anything to offend, you tell me straight off. Her Grace has put you in my charge and I don't let my girls be mauled about. Remember that."

Opal gave her promise and was introduced to Jed, Hockey and Dick, the barmen, and Saul Tysoe, who was in charge of the cellars.

Then the miracle happened. Mrs. Dabbs was shewing Opal the kitchen and where to find the pots and pans, when the door opened there was Susie Phelps. The two girls stared at each other for a moment. Then with a cry of delight they ran into each other's arms.

When Alice heard of their former friendship she was well pleased.

"Good. Best for girls of your age to have a pal. You can look out for each other. Susie, make Opal a cup of tea and give her some sandwiches. Then you can shew her where she's going to sleep."

"In my room?" Susie was still overcome. "Mrs. Dabbs, may she sleep with me?"

"Where else?" Alice gave a click of impatience. "This isn't an hotel, you know. Bedrooms have to be shared like everything else around here."

"She's a dear really," said Susie when Mrs. Dabbs had gone. "Sometimes she pretends to be fierce, but that's only 'cos she's got to keep things running by herself since her husband died. Opal, it's so wonderful to see you again. There's so much I want to tell you and you'll have to give me all your news as well. Have you seen Davey since he left Lockgate?"

"No, don't suppose we ever will, do you? He could be anywhere. He might even have gone to sea."

"No, he won't have done that. Always said he hated the sea. He'll be making money somewhere, you can bet on that. It would be nice if we did meet him some day, wouldn't it?"

Opal thought of the boy who had protected her from bullies and dared her to sing the song which had landed her in The Death Hole. She didn't hold any grudges on the latter score. It had been worth it just to see the approval in Campbell's eyes when she had emerged, her head unbowed.

"Yes it would. Well, we can but hope. Now, what about those sandwiches? I had a meal earlier but that seems ages ago and I've done a lot of walking since then."

"Of course, I'll do them straight away. You don't know how glad I am you're here. I think this is one of the happiest days of my life."

"Mine, too." Opal gave Susie a kiss. "This is my starting-point; my first real chance and I'm not going to muff it. I won't always be doing my turn in a pub in the East End. I'm going right to the top, and, what's more, I'm taking you with me."

Susie was buttering thick slices of fresh bread, her hands stilled for a moment by Opal's words.

"You mean it? You'll let me come, too?"

"I mean it. Now that I've found you I'll make sure we aren't parted any more. Oh, Susie, Susie, one day we're both going to be madly rich and famous and our names will be on everyone's lips. Meanwhile, how about hurrying up that food, there's a dear. I know it's awful, but I'm starving again."

Five

At the end of six months, Alice Dabbs found that Opal had become almost indispensable.

Not only did she do more than her fair share of the humdrum chores; she had also captured the imagination and the hearts of those who frequented the tavern.

Opal had known from the first that she would have to make up her mind what kind of performer she would be. She had to choose a distinctive act, working on it until it was all her own. She could have sung ballads; her voice was good enough. Her dancing could have been ethereal and graceful, for she was as light on her feet as thistledown.

In the end she decided against that path, for it smacked too much of the legitimate theatre and she had set her sights on the music halls. She concentrated on rather saucy songs, but she put them over with such an innocent air that she convinced everyone, except Alice, that she really had no idea what the naughty innuendoes meant.

She had used some of the money Ivy had given her to provide herself and Susie with appropriate costumes. With her tongue in her cheek she had stitched away at a dress suitable for a child of twelve. She curled her hair into ringlets and covered her mouth with lip-salve until it looked like a small girl's pout.

Her dancing was as audacious as her ditties. Her steps were quick and lively, and she used her body to convey more than the lyrics could ever do, tossing her skirts up as she finished. The applause deafened the two musicians playing for her, but warmed the cockles of her own heart. She had found her métier, and all she had to do was to practise until she dropped.

Susie couldn't dance to save her life, but Opal persuaded Alice to let the girl try a song or two. Dressed in rags and barefoot, Susie piped away at the most heart-rending numbers which had half her listeners in tears. Even the most hardened of men wanted to protect and cosset the pathetic waif.

Alice grumbled, saying the people would think she didn't give Susie enough to eat, but when she totted up her takings at the end of each week she had to admit that the presence of the two girls made a difference.

It was Alice who got hold of the songs for Opal and Susie. She had contacts with a man on the halls who owed her several favours. Sheets of music and verse came in a flood and there was never any lack of material.

One elderly and passionate devotee of *Barney's Ale House* was Sidney Bannerman. He took a great fancy to Opal from the first, presenting her with bouquets of flowers, chocolates and other small gift.

"Keep your hands to yourself, Sid," said Alice, who had eyes like a hawk. "Bits and pieces yes, but nothing expensive d'you hear? And you're not going to see Opal alone, so put that in your pipe and smoke it."

While Bannerman drooled over Opal, she was thinking of Edward. Not all the time, of course, for she was far too busy. It was at night, when she and Susie had settled down to sleep, that the earl's face came floating down from nowhere to torment her. After their second meeting he didn't bring comfort; just a hollow ache because he was beyond her reach.

It was on Opal's sixteenth birthday that Alice made a decision which, as she said many times afterwards, was her own undoing. Opal had continued to press Alice for details of *The Canterbury Hall,* and when the latter was in a good mood she would talk about it, watching the yearning in Opal's eyes. Because they'd been so good for business, Alice decided to take Opal and Susie to *The Canterbury Hall* as a birthday treat

All three of them got dressed up, and Sidney Bannerman was permitted the signal honour of escorting them. "Can't go without a man," Alice had said reluctantly. "He'll do and he can pay for his own meal."

Opal and Susie were reduced to silence as they were led through a brightly-lit entrance, up some steps, and into the main hall. It was a vast place which could seat fifteen hundred people with ease, and above it was a balcony with panelled fronts. Opposite the curve of the horseshoe was a stage, with harmonium and piano. The Chairman in charge of that evening's procedures was sitting beneath it, glass in hand, a cigar stuck between his teeth.

There were countless tables and chairs, pillars and archways, ornamental brackets holding several gas-lamps each and a huge chandelier made of lustrous glass hanging from the ceiling.

When the girls at last found their voices they chorused their amazement at the size and splendour of the place, Opal twisting and turning and not missing a thing which was going on about her.

Then came the food. A favourite dish at *The Canterbury* was baked potatoes in their jackets. Opal watched one of the waiters take the red-hot vegetable in a white cloth, bursting it open, and placing a generous blob of butter in its floury centre. It was a far cry from the potato vendors of Raven Court, and Opal could hardly wait for hers to be served.

Of course there was much else to tempt the palate. Chops and steaks, sausages cooked to a turn, kidneys, bacon, scrambled eggs and oysters were but a few of the delicacies from which Charles Morton's patrons could take their pick.

"That's Morton," said Alice as she stabbed her fork into a pork chop. "See, he's serving his special cronies with the potatoes. Just watch the neat way he does it. His motto's 'One Quality Only, the Best.' Spruce, isn't he? Have to admit it, he's the cleverest in the business. He's got rivals, naturally, but none can touch him."

"I'd love to meet him." Opal neglected her eggs and bacon to concentrate on the Father of the Halls. "Do you think I will one day?"

Alice shrugged.

"Maybe, if things go your way. Talent isn't enough, you know. You need luck as well."

It was less than a week later that Opal put her first ideas to Alice.

"Polished tables in the free-and-easy?"

"We could rename it the Club Room and we could have brass candlesticks and proper wax candles which don't smoke."

Alice was outraged.

"Oh, could we, Miss? And what else does her highness think of doing?"

"Buying good-quality glasses, decorating the walls and hanging some pictures."

"Sake's alive! I suppose you want pile carpet and velvet curtains as well?"

"No." Opal's enthusiasm was undimmed by Mrs. Dabbs' sarcasm. "But we could get some spills and put them in pewter tankards."

Before Opal could get any more ludicrous ideas, Alice stepped in with brisk common sense.

"And where, pray, are we going to get the money for all this?"

"From your extra takings for the time being. But once the place is put to rights you'll have far more customers coming in, so you won't lose."

Alice objected and spluttered her rage for twenty-four hours. Then Opal, Susie and Jed went to the market to see what they could find. Jed, as head barman, was in favour of the idea and had a few thoughts of how he could improve the main part of the tavern into the bargain.

Opal's prophecy came true. More men did frequent the new Club Room and Alice's income rose yet again. When she was seventeen, Opal sprang her next surprise on the unfortunate Mrs. Dabbs.

"What! Serve food here? You're mad, girl."

"I wasn't mad over the Club Room, was I?"

"That was different."

"Not really. We wouldn't have to have as many dishes as they serve at *The Canterbury*, of course. We should specialise, like other song and supper-rooms do."

"This isn't a song and supper-room, you featherhead. It's an ordinary pub in Whitechapel."

"It is now, but it could become the most famous place in the East End. I think we ought to have potatoes in their jackets, like Mr. Morton does. They're cheap and filling, and everyone seems to like them. Apart from them, we could have winkles instead of oysters, and pork sausages with onion gravy."

"We'll do no such thing," snapped the exasperated Alice. "You've got a sight too big for your boots, just 'cos the customers like you. I'm not having my tavern turned into a dandy's den. No food and no song and supper-room, and that's flat."

Alice's defeat came a week or two later. She wasn't sure why she capitulated, unless it was because she had grown so fond of Opal. She held out as long as she could, but within a month a cook and a scullery-maid had been hired and tables and chairs purchased.

The reaction of the locals was amazing, at least to Alice. They brought their womenfolk and they lapped up Opal's jacket-potatoes and sausages as if they'd never tasted anything like them in their lives.

A week before Opal's eighteenth birthday, Alice said cautiously:

"You haven't got anything else daft in mind, have you? Seems to me you're at your worst when your birthday's coming up."

Opal smiled serenely, safe in the knowledge that Alice was putty in her hands and that she was wrapped around with Mrs. Dabbs' affection.

"Matter of a fact I have."

"Oh Gawd! I knew it. Well, let's hear it. Jed, get me a brandy; I think I'm going to need it."

A few days later workmen arrived to tear down the back wall of the tavern and incorporate into the dining-area several back rooms, thus providing space for another twenty tables.

"We don't need all those stores," said Opal as Alice wrung her hands. "Think of the money you're going to make when the work's finished."

Alice gave up, and by the time Opal was nineteen there was little improvement to be made to *Barney's Ale House*. There were bill-posts outside announcing the menu, and Opal and Susie weren't the only entertainers by then. Acrobats and conjurers were hired from time to time; a good tenor or a would-be opera singer came to warble airs of a more classical nature.

But the main drawing-power of Alice's tavern was Opal. She had grown more beautiful than ever, and her professionalism was beyond doubt. She devoured songs as others scoffed brown beer, and the twinkle in her eyes had grown more mischievous still.

The people of Whitechapel and surrounding areas adored her. They were very proud of having a proper song and supper-room on their doorstep, and even more delighted to have an entertainer of Opal's quality. Young men wooed her, in vain; older men sighed for her.

The women were just as smitten. She wasn't a threat to them, for she didn't want their husbands and lovers. She seemed to them to be singing to her own sex, gently mocking the follies of the male of the specie, but confirming with a wink that neither she nor her sisters-under-the-skin could do without them.

One day, news of the metamorphosis of *Barney's Ale House* reached the ears of Mr. Herbert Finn, manager and owner of *Finn's Music Hall* in Holborn. He was always on the look-out for new talent, and, from what he'd been told,

Miss Shannon was something special. Although her fame was limited at present, it might not be long before Morton heard about her, too, and Herbert decided to get in first if he could.

He was impressed by the tavern; rumour hadn't lied. He was served with sausages from a spotlessly clean dish, the knife and fork beside his plate polished to perfection. The food was excellent, the beer strong. Jed and the other barmen, who helped out as waiters, were courteous without being subservient. He was made to feel that he mattered, but, equally, that he was fortunate to have found a free table on such a busy night.

The stories about Opal weren't exaggerated. He knew the second she started her first number that she was a winner and all that remained to be done was for him to steal her away from Alice Dabbs.

But when Herbert met Alice he felt an unexpected jolt. His wife had died years before and he'd never bothered about women after that, except for a bit of fun now and then. But the tiny woman with neatly-dressed hair and a gown fit for a royal reception made him feel like a callow schoolboy, and he hardly knew what to say to her, never mind introducing the subject of larceny as far as Miss Shannon was concerned.

It was the same for Alice, but she was more self-possessed about it. She hadn't wanted another man after Barney, but there was something about the tall, broad-shouldered man with grey hair and a military manner which made her feel quite excited.

Calmly, she invited him into her private parlour, plying him with cognac. She had always found that was the best thing to loosen the tongue, and she wanted to know much more about Finn.

He found himself telling her all about his early days and how he had managed to get the music hall in Holborn started. Alice listened, but didn't say much. Men didn't like women who interrupted them with remarks of their own.

"I've got a confession to make," said Herbert, mopping his brow as he caught sight of Alice's ankle. "I'm a fool to tell you, but somehow I've got to be honest with you."

Alice smiled soothingly.

"I don't bite. You can tell me, whatever it is."

"You won't throw me out?"

"I doubt it." Alice had no intention of doing any such thing, tightening her hold on Herbert with subtle sweetness. "Do go on."

"I didn't come here to-night just to have a meal."

"No?"

"No, although it was excellent and I congratulate you on your place. Never thought I'd find anything like this in Whitechapel."

"Don't suppose you did, but if it had been left to me it would still be a pot-house like it was when my husband was alive. Miss Shannon made me do the alterations. I took her to *The Canterbury Hall* and paid dearly for it."

Finn raised his eyebrows.

"Miss Shannon?"

"Yes. All the changes and the serving of food were her idea. I wonder she didn't make a pauper of me."

"I'm sure you've doubled your takings."

"Trebled them or more, actually. Mr. Finn, let's get down to brass tacks, shall we? Someone told you about Opal, didn't they?"

"Shrewd as well as pretty, Mrs. Dabbs."

A delicious shiver ran through Alice, but it didn't put her off the main issue.

"Want her for your own hall, I suppose?"

"She'd make her name there. A real artiste, that one. Nothing vulgar in her, but her songs'll drive my audiences wild. They like a bit of smut, you see, provided it's dished up in the right way. Any chance of us coming to some kind of agreement?"

Alice's smile made Herbert sweat again.

"There might be, Mr. Finn. Naturally we'd have to talk it over thoroughly, I'm sure you realise that. Mean you calling here a time or two. I can't come up to Holborn."

"I'll come." Herbert said it with such rapidity that Alice knew for certain that she'd hooked him. "I'll be here as often as I can get away. To talk things over, of course."

"Of course. I think you'll find it'll be worth your while."

"So do I," replied Herbert fervently. "To-morrow?"

"If it isn't too much to ask. We might begin to discuss the preliminaries, so to speak."

When he had gone Alice went over to the mirror and looked at herself thoughtfully. Her cheeks were quite pink, and not because she'd used any rouge. The eyes sparkled like diamonds, and she laughed aloud.

"Alice, my girl, you're a hussy. Poor Mr. Finn; I wonder if he realises exactly what to-night's visit is going to cost him."

* * *

The following evening was wet and cold. Opal and Susie had just finished their respective numbers when they heard Jed's voice raised in anger.

"Jed? What is it?"

"It's this cove, Miss Opal. Looks like a tramp to me. Says 'e wants a job, but I reckon 'e's mind on thievin'. Don't belong in a respectable establishment like this, and 'e burstin' in as if 'e owned the place."

Opal looked at the thin young man and felt instant compassion. There was a deep sadness in him which had nothing to do with the wet rags he was wearing, nor the gauntness of his cheeks. His dark eyes were filled with pain and he was actuely embarrassed by Jed's accusation.

"Oh, Jed, no! How can you say such a thing?"

Opal turned to look at Susie and felt a grue. She understood the way Susie was looking at the stranger; it was the way she had looked at Edward Adare. Then she turned back to the newcomer, only to find his expression had altered completely. He was gazing at Susie as if he wanted to eat her.

Opal couldn't stop the nagging fear clutching at her heart. Somehow she knew that Susie and the man were going to love deeply and that a black cloud would hover over them each day they were together. There wasn't going to be a happy ending for Susie, any more than there would be one for her. Then she shook the nonsense out of herself.

"What's your name?"

"Johnny Dibell, and I didn't come to steal. I really do want to work."

"What do you do?"

"I'm a comic."

Anyone less like a comedian Opal had yet to see, but she kept her doubts to herself. Susie was like one in a trance, and Dibell barely took his eyes off her as he answered the question.

"Don't you bother any more, Jed." Opal gave the barman a dismissive nod. "I'll see to this. Well, Johnny Dibell, we'd better find you some dry clothes from somewhere, and you look hungry to me."

His grin was endearing, and Opal's worries increased. Susie would never be able to resist him when he looked like that. She said briskly:

"Susie, go and get some hot soup and bread and cheese ready. Mr. Dibell, come with me. I'll find you something to wear."

After Dibell had eaten his first meal for three days he sank back in his chair with a sigh.

"You're very kind to me, both of you. I can't pay for this."

"You don't have to." Susie was swift to reassure him. "You're our guest."

"Only until we see what Alice says about Mr. Dibell working here." Opal tried to warn her friend, but she knew she was wasting her breath. The harm was already done. "You'd better meet Mrs. Dabbs now. I'll take you to her."

Alice was having a port and lemon in her parlour, none too pleased at having her brief sit-down interrupted.

She listened to Opal, glancing at Susie's wrapt face as she did so.

"And he wants to do a turn here, Alice." Susie's hands were clasped together in entreaty. "You will let him, won't you?"

Mrs. Dabbs and Opal exchanged a pregnant look. They both knew what had happened, for Johnny's eyes were lit up just like Susie's.

"Depends if he's any good."

"I'm sure he is, but he's tired now. He's been on the road for three days and hadn't had a bite to eat until we gave him something. Please, please say you'll give him a chance."

Alice took another sip. She was a kind-hearted woman and was nearly as fond of Susie as she was of Opal. The boy, for he wasn't much more, looked like a skeleton. It wasn't likely that he'd make anyone laugh, but she couldn't turn him away without a hearing.

"All right. Come back to-morrow morning, Mr. Dibell, and we'll see what you've got up your sleeve. Found somewhere to stay tonight, have you?"

"Yes, Mrs. Dabbs, I'm fixed up right enough."

"Liar."

He flushed, out of countenance again because he knew what a wretched spectacle he must appear to the well-dressed Mrs. Dabbs.

"I'll manage."

"And get that suit wet as well. Dick's, isn't it?"

"He didn't mind." Susie flew to Johnny's defence as if Alice was attacking him physically. "We did ask first."

"I should hope so. Well, no point in getting soaked again. Opal, tell Saul to fix Mr. Dibell up with a bed in the cellar. Sorry we haven't anything else to offer you, but it's warm and dry down there."

Johnny's gratitude had the same effect on Alice as it had done on Opal.

"No need to thank me that much. It's little enough, heaven knows. Opal, when you and Susie and Saul have got things settled, I'd like a word with you."

"You know what's happened, don't you?" asked Alice some twenty minutes late. "That silly girl's gone and fallen in love. Never believed in love at first sight myself, but it seems I was wrong."

"Yes, it can happen." Opal was very quiet. "I can vouch for that."

"Never got over him, have you? The earl, I mean. Meant to ask you about that once or twice. Then I thought I'd best keep my mouth shut. Still, back to Susie. She's only a kid, and what about him?"

"He feels the same."

"Lor', what a fine kettle of fish. I hope he's useless so I can send him packing."

"She'd go, too."

"Reckon she would. However bad he is, Mr. Dibell will have to stay on for a while until we can cure that ninny."

"There's no cure for being in love."

"Judging by you, I suppose there isn't. I wish you could meet someone else. Don't like to think of you wasting your life away."

"There couldn't be anyone except Edward."

"But you'll never see him again."

"Probably not."

"Well, then, a girl like you left on the shelf. It isn't right."

"Right or wrong, that's how 's going to be. Oh, Alice, why do women have to be born with such foolish hearts?"

* * *

"You've asked Gillian Wintour to marry you? You must be mad!"

Edward wasn't surprised that his grandmother was raising objections. He had proposed to Gillian on the spur of the moment, not because he was in love with her but because he knew he had to have an heir.

There was another reason, too. The memory of the girl who had sung and danced for him still came back to him far more often than it should have done. Four years was a long time, and he'd only talked to her for ten minutes at most. He had to drive her from his heart and mind once and for all, and Gillian was the one he'd selected to do his emotional spring-cleaning for him.

"You're only annoyed because I didn't discuss the matter with you first. I suppose I ought to have done, but she was at Lord Croft's ball the night before last and there seemed no point in waiting any longer. We've seen quite a lot of each other recently. She's beautiful, and even you can't find fault with her lineage."

The duchess was older. Many more wrinkles puckered up soft skin which had been like alabaster in her youth. Her hair was thinning and she never let anyone but Doris Whicker see her without a lace cap on top of her head. Her lips were no longer pink, and tiny lines ran from them, emphasising the passing years. Her hands, once so slim and white, were crooked with rheumatism, brown spots like freckles on the backs of them.

Only her eyes and her spirit remained untouched by time. Those and her sharp tongue which she was now using to shew her disapproval.

"She may be beautiful, but she's like Clio. I noticed that on the first occasion I met her. That's what attracts you to her. You're still clinging to the dead. Edward, let them go."

"I think I have." The earl gave Annice a quick smile. "It wasn't easy, but I can remember them now without pain. Do you really think Gillian is like Clio was?"

"Of course she is. Anyone who'd known them both would have to be blind not to see it. Are you sure it isn't too late to withdraw from this betrothal?"

"Quite sure. I asked her to be my wife, and she accepted me, so did her mother."

"Of course she did. The Wintours are penniless. After her husband died Lady Wintour found he had left nothing but debts. That's why the girl consented."

"Oh come, Annie. Am I so unattractive that Gillian can only be considering my financial status? Can't you accept that she might be fond of me?"

"Certainly not. Don't be such a blockhead. That creature cares for no one but herself. No doubt she's glad you're handsome as well as wealthy, but love! Don't delude yourself, Edward, you're being used."

"It doesn't really matter much, does it? You said after the accident that I needed an heir. Gillian looks healthy."

"So she is, but you could have looked further than a robust brood-mare. Don't pretend you have any deep feelings for her because I won't believe it. If all you want is a mother for your children, there are plenty of other wenches with sweeter dispositions than that one. Well-born she may be, but she's also a frivolous, lightminded little madam. selfish to the core."

Kynston didn't deny the accusation, and the duchess's voice softened.

"There's another woman, isn't there? That's why you rushed into this nonsensical match like a bull in a china shop. If you really thought your decision was a right one, you'd have talked to me first. You're running away from someone. Who is it?"

"You'd think me insane if I told you."

"I've already said you're mad to couple yourself with the Wintour filly. I've seen the sadness in you when you were off-guard. She must be very dear to you."

"She is, but I can't have her. I must forget her if I'm to survive. Marriage is the answer."

"Marriage with Gillian Wintour is an answer, but it's the wrong one. However, there's nothing we can do about it now. You've made your bed of thorns; now you'll have to lie on it. Tell me about her; the other one, I mean."

"It's so ludicrous that you'd laugh."

"Not about the woman you love, Edward, never that."

"I only saw her twice. Once, a long time ago, in Regent

Street. She gave me back my pocket-book. Then I saw her outside this house; she was looking for work as a kitchen-maid."

Annice closed her eyes. Her intuition had been right. She'd sent Opal Shannon to Mrs. Dabbs' tavern to get her out of Edward's sight, but her move had been too late.

"Are you shocked?"

The duchess shook her head.

"Not in the least. She was utterly delightful; that's why I got rid of her."

"You saw her? When – how – "

"You told her to ask Mrs. Palmer for a position. I understand that you even shewed her where the servants' entrance was. Whicker had seen you with the girl; she watched her dance and sing. I sent for Miss Shannon."

Edward was shaken.

"I'd no idea."

"Of course you hadn't; I made sure of that. As soon as she began to talk to me I knew what had made you happy for the first time since the ship went down. Whicker heard your laughter, too, you see. I sent your Opal to a place where I knew she'd be cared for."

"May I know to whom you sent her?"

"Emphatically not."

Edward took a seat opposite his grandmother.

"Did you guess what I felt about her?"

"I wasn't quite sure, but I couldn't take any chances. The trouble was that although she was so young she was in love with you. She told me she'd dreamed of you since that afternoon in Regent Street. She accepted that nothing could come of it. She was sensible and very courageous. I'm not going to let you see her and upset the life she's made for herself."

"No." Edward was looking down at his hands. "That wouldn't be fair, would it? I love her, Annie, I always will. As you say, she was no age, but somehow that didn't seem to matter. I'd have waited fifty years for her if I'd thought I'd had a chance."

"But you have no chance." Annice was as compassionate as she'd been with Opal. "How damnably ridiculous our conventions are. So much love wasted because you're a nobleman and she's from the slums. I'm sorry, Edward, truly sorry."

"Thank you. I'm glad you know; it makes it feel less of a burden. You see now why I must marry?"

"I see you need a wife, you've always needed one, but not the one you've picked. Still, as I've said, the harm's done. I'll write to Lady Wintour and ask her to call on me. I wish I could buy happiness for you as once I bought you horses."

"So do I. It's good of you not to shout at me about something you can't really understand."

Annice was very tart.

"I never shout, and as for understanding, you nincompoop, I know as much about unrequited love as you do. I was eighteen and would have died for the man in question. My father said he wasn't suitable and I was packed off to Paris. I never saw my dear one again. I think he left England, too, because he felt as I did. I married your grandfather and I was happy enough, but it wasn't the real thing."

"Oh God! I'm ten times worse than a bull in a china shop."

The duchess's brief irritation was done as she leaned forward to pat the earl's arm.

"Don't blame yourself; you didn't know about my tale of woe. I shouldn't have mentioned it. I've only made things worse. Oh, Edward my dear, what an unlucky pair we are. Now get me a glass of Madeira, and quickly, or I shall start to cry."

* * *

"Gillian, I saw you making eyes at Beamish again this afternoon when we returned from shopping. How can you demean yourself so? He's a common coachman."

The Hon. Gillian Wintour as studying herself in the mirror. It was one of her favourite pastimes, and the reflection thrown back never failed to please her.

Her dark hair was brushed back from her forehead, puffed out round her ears and then captured in a chignon at the nape of her neck. Her eyes were deep brown and luminous, her complexion like milk, her lips full and sensual. She had a sparkling vivacity which attracted many men in her circle. She responded with smiles which hinted of promises she'd no intention of making good, and a blush she seemed able to produce at will.

"Don't fuss, mama. You're quite mistaken anyway."

Lady Elizabeth Wintour hadn't been in error as Gillian knew full well. She had accepted Kynston because she wanted his name and his fortune, but it was coarse brutes like the coachman who made her tingle in odd, unexpected places.

She had seen Beamish strip her naked with a glance, wondering what his strong, calloused hands would feel like on her body. He had seemed even bolder that day, and the mere remembrance of his suggestive look made her go hot all over.

"I'm not mistaken. You can't afford a scandal. Do you want to lose Adare?"

"I shan't lose him. It's too late for him to change his mind." Gillian was fastening an emerald necklace round her throat, a gift from Edward. "I've snared him; you needn't worry."

"I can't help it. And it's not only your absurd flirtations. You're sending the earl far too many bills to pay. He may think twice about taking such an extravagant woman for his wife."

"He can think about it a hundred times." Gillian was offhand. "I've just told you; he can't back out of it now."

She rose, admiring her ball dress of pink tulle over an underskirt of ruched satin. The bodice was cut low off the shoulders, a fashion of which she heartily approved. She wished she could slip down to the stables where Beamish and the groom were having their supper. She wanted to drive the coachman mad with desire to pay him back for what he'd done to her.

"Well, I hope you're right. Are you in love with the earl?"

Gillian threw back her head and laughed.

"Mama, how funny you are. Of course I'm not and he's not in love with me. I've heard all about his mistresses."

"Men of his kind always have mistresses. Your father did, but I had to put up with it. It'll be the same for you. You'll have to give in to him, even if he isn't faithful."

"I don't mind opening my legs for Edward, provided I can have some fun, too."

"What an unutterably crude thing to say!"

"It's the normal way to copulate."

Lady Wintour covered her ears in horror.

"I won't listen to you. You're disgusting."

"No, just honest. You don't like looking at things as they really are, do you?"

"I won't discuss the matter any further. I'm sure that Edward is very fond of you. Why else would he ask you to marry him?"

"Because he wants a son, as beautiful as I am. I don't care if he hates the sight of me as long as he gives me all I ask for and isn't tiresome about my lovers."

"You – you haven't – "

"Not yet, but I'm going to. As for Edward's mistresses, I'm glad he's had some practise. I don't want a virgin husband who fumbles all over me and can't give me satisfaction."

Lady Wintour sat down on the edge of the bed and began to cry.

"For heaven's sake! What's wrong with you now?"

"I'm so afraid something may stop this marriage. We're nearly bankrupt. I haven't even got enough to pay the tradesmen and they're refusing to let us have any further goods."

"Is that all?" Gillian opened a drawer in her dressing-table and threw a velvet purse into Elizabeth's lap. "Here, give them that. It'll keep them from howling at our doors for a while."

Lady Wintour stared at the sovereigns.

"So much! Where did you get it from?"

"From Edward, of course. I explained how dire our straits were and he was very generous. I shall ask him for some more to-night."

"Should you? Won't he think – "

"Of course I should. You've just said we'll starve if we can't settle our accounts. And, mother – "

The tone of Gillian's voice changed completely, and she had never called Lady Wintour 'mother' before.

Elizabeth looked up, her apprehension increasing as she saw a new and quite unexpected hardness in her daughter.

"Yes, what is it?"

"Don't keep nagging me, either about Beamish or my language. It bores me and you wouldn't want to upset me, would you? When I'm the Countess of Kynston I shall be very rich indeed. You expect me to look after you in your old age, don't you?"

Elizabeth was shocked into silence. The thought that some share of Kynston's wealth would come her way had buoyed up her spirits through the difficulties of the past year. She had been triumphant when she had secured the earl for her daughter, snatching him away from her envious friends who had hoped to get him for their own offspring. She had seen her future secure, lacking nothing, and the mother-in-law of one of society's darlings.

The Gillian she had pushed, pulled and bullied for most of the former's life seemed to have vanished in a split second. In her place was an arrogant young woman who had the upper hand, and a very powerful hand at that.

Lady Wintour's mouth grew dry, not knowing what to say to the stranger looking down at her.

"Well – yes. I had thought you'd see that I had a proper

income of my own. After all, you owe me a lot."

"I owe you nothing. I didn't ask to be born, and ever since I was old enough to put on the marriage market you've used me to try to feather a comfortable nest for yourself. You weren't thinking of me at all. You've never thought about me and what I want."

"That's not true! Why are you being so unkind?"

"I'm not, I'm being truthful again. I'll make a pact with you. I'll be generous if you stop treating me like a child and criticising everything I say and do. And you'd better make up your mind here and now or you may find it's too late."

There was a long silence during which it seemed to Lady Wintour that she and her daughter were changing places. Gillian was the dominant one now; she, Elizabeth, the child who had to obey. She swallowed her defeat like a bitter pill.

"Very well, if that is your wish."

"It's more than a mere wish. Do we understand each other?"

Lady Wintour knew that her nose was being rubbed in her submission, but there was nothing she could do about it. It had all happened so quickly that she hadn't had time to build defences. But there was no mistaking Gillian's unwavering stare, and she did her best to reply with what was left of her dignity.

"Yes, we do."

"Good, that's settled. Now, tell me how I look."

"You look beautiful."

It wasn't enough. Gillian was demanding a better return on the money she had given her mother and a stronger indication that things were going to be different from then on.

"And?"

Elizabeth knew it was just the first of many humiliations which she would have to endure in the days to come, but the alternative to pandering to her daughter didn't bear thinking about.

She let go the last of her self-respect, accepting her lot with a heavy heart.

"And – and any man would be proud to marry you. The Earl of Kynston is a very lucky man, dear. Yes, he really is very lucky indeed."

Six

On a bright April afternoon, Opal went to the West End to buy some material for a dress. Although Alice paid her generously, Opal never wasted money; she had lived too intimately with poverty for that. She put most of her earnings in the bank, but now and then, because she was nineteen and liked to look her best, she bought a new shawl, a pair of shoes or a bonnet.

Normally she went to the local market, but for once she was restless and wanted to look further than the boundaries of East London.

She hadn't meant to go to Grosvenor Square. She had tried not to think about it on her journey, but it was no good. Her feet seemed to have a will of their own, and she found herself staring up at Edward's home, wondering if he were there.

"Are you still looking for a position as a kitchen-maid?"

Opal felt her heart begin to thud, yet there was a certain inevitability about their meeting. She had known that some time and in some place she would see Edward again, no matter how often common sense told her that that was impossible.

When she turned to look at him she felt a strange sense of peace. Her memory had served her well. Nothing about him had changed, and his smile almost took her breath away.

While Opal was trying to find the right words, Kynston had the opportunity of studying the face which had become as familiar to him as his own. The eyes were still as blue as the summer sky; her hair glinted like pure gold under the chip hat she wore. Only her body had changed. She was no longer a girl of fifteen. She was a woman, and Nature had given her curves which made the blood race in his veins.

At last Opal found her tongue.

"I'm sorry, my lord. You must think it very peculiar that I am gawping at your house like this."

Her voice was soft and full of music, bemusing his senses.

"No, but I hope you'll tell me the true reason why you're here"

"I'd feel even more stupid if I had to make a full confession."

"You know that isn't so, but if it makes it easier for you I'll tell you something. I have waited four long years for this. Was it the same for you? Is that why you came?"

There was no point in denying it. In any event, Opal had never been a good liar.

"Yes, it was the same for me. I did try to forget all about you, but I couldn't. I promised myself I'd never come here again, but to-day it was different."

"We can't talk here."

"Where can we go?"

"I know somewhere. We'll get a cab."

When they were seated at a table in Pavini's, a small retreat for those who didn't want to be seen in popular restaurants like Gunters', the earl said:

"Tell me what you've been doing."

"It's rather a long story."

"That doesn't matter. Will you pour? I can recommend the shortbread; it's very good. Are you a music hall artiste yet?"

Opal picked up the pot, hoping her hand wouldn't shake. Things had happened with such bewildering speed that she felt as if she were caught up in a whirlpool.

"No, but I'm hoping to be one quite soon. You see, after I left you that day the duchess gave me a letter to Alice Dabbs – "

He listened without interrupting, content to be with her and drink in her beauty. When her tale was finished she blushed.

"I'm sorry. I've talked too much about myself. I must have wearied you."

Their eyes met, and he said quietly:

"We haven't time to pretend, you and I. I'm engaged to be married, but the wedding won't be for some months. Are you willing to share those months with me?"

Opal knew she ought to refuse. Edward didn't belong to her; he was promised to another woman. Perhaps Fate had designed the crossing of their paths once more, but it was a temptation which should be rejected. On the other hand, the only real life she would ever have would be with the man sitting opposite her. The rest would be a mere existence.

Being with him, touching his hand, feeling his lips against hers, would make the final parting so much harder, but she couldn't resist the unspoken plea in him. She didn't want to resist; she wanted to be in his arms.

"I'd like that."

"I love you and I kept my promise. I said I'd think of you every day. Do you remember? It was when you sang for me."

"I remember, and I love you, too. I think I first realised that when I saw you in Regent Street, although I was only nine."

"You were so small and dreadfully cold. I wished I could have put my coat round you."

"How kind you are, but my brother had stolen your pocket-book."

"And you'd returned it to me. We've had such brief meetings, yet you mean so much to me. Do you realise how painful it will be when our *affaire* is over? I wouldn't hurt you for the world, so if – "

"I know how it will be. It'll be awful for both of us, but that's the price we'll have to pay for our happiness. I'm prepared to settle the account in full. Are you?"

"Down to the last ha'penny. Dear Opal, how very lovely you are. We must see each other soon. Will you have difficulty in getting away?"

"No, Alice lets me have every Monday and Thursday afternoon off, and she never asks questions."

"Sweet, understanding Alice. I would like to embrace her because she knows how to mind her own business. And I would like to kiss you."

"That might cause a few heads to turn." Her hand rested on the table until her finger-tips met his. "We will have to be patient."

"I suppose so. I'll buy a house as soon as I can. Please don't think I'm ashamed of what I feel for you, but I have to use discretion in my choice of property."

She gave a small laugh, comforting him.

"I didn't expect you to get one next door to your own. What would your grandmother say? She thought she'd seen the last of me."

"She knows how I feel about you; I told her."

"She must have been very angry."

"No she wasn't, not about that. She was very understanding as it happens. She didn't like my choice of bride and told me so in no uncertain terms what she thought of Gillian Wintour."

"Is she beautiful?"

"Gillian? Yes, I suppose so, but not as you are. It's a marriage of convenience, nothing more. I have to have a son."

"Yes, I do understand. Suppose the duchess finds out about us?"

"I'm sure she will. Nothing much escapes her."

"Will she try to stop you seeing me?"

"She can't; she's no longer my guardian. I think if she does discover what's going on she'll know why it has to be. Did you like her when you saw her that day?"

"Yes I did, and I don't want to cause trouble between you."

"You won't. Annie found herself in much the same boat when she was a girl. She won't judge us too harshly."

"How odd all this is. When I got up at six o'clock this morning I'd no idea it was going to be the most important day of my life. I helped Susie with the vegetables, washed a lot of glasses and then polished the tables in the Club Room. I set out to buy some material for a dress, but instead I found you."

"My day was just as ordinary until I saw you in Grosvenor Square. I had begun to think the miracle would never happen, but there you were."

"I can't understand why I'm being such a forward hussy. Why aren't I blushing and making coy protestations at your improper advances?"

"Because real love leaves no room for such things. It's all-consuming and, as we know, can flourish in very barren soil. The four years felt like forty, but the love never grew weak."

"Are you afraid of it?"

"Only of its ending."

"We won't think about that. We have to cram everything which matters to us into weeks instead of years. We won't squander a second worrying about the future. And now I must go, for I still have to do my shopping. If I returned to the tavern empty-handed even Alice would smell a rat. No, don't come with me. You might be recognised."

Edward rose, standing as close to her as he dared.

"I wish it didn't have to be like this for you."

"But it is. That's one of the items on the bill. Next Thursday, here, at three?"

Opal didn't look back, but made her way to a draper's shop, the blue silk, green satin, yellow velvet and red brocade merging together until all she could see was Edward's face.

She chose at random, and the young man serving her began to regard her with some suspicion. Usually, females hummed and hawed for half an hour or more before they made up their minds what they wanted. The girl with the smile on her lips and dreams in her eyes didn't seem to care what she bought.

When Opal saw the assistant's expression she began to see the funny side of it. Ten minutes ago she had agreed to become Edward Adare's mistress and joy was flooding through her in a torrent. There had been no awkwardness between them as one might expect. She felt as though they had spent part of every day of their lives together and knew he felt the same. It was as Edward had said; real love was strong and could overcome anything. Her world had changed in a few minutes, yet here she was mooning over bits of cloth, the salesman clearly of the opinion that she wasn't right in the head. She thought perhaps he might be right. There was a measure of madness in what she'd done.

She kept her face very straight as she took the parcel with a gracious nod.

"Thank you so much. I'm very pleased with this, whatever it is. I think it will make a most becoming shroud."

Then she left the shop quickly, running down Regent Street like a bird let out of a cage, just managing to catch the horse-omnibus which would take her back to Whitechapel and reality.

* * *

A few days after Opal's meeting with the earl, Herbert announced that he was prepared to give Opal and Susie a spot on his bill at *Finn's Music Hall*.

Opal was over the moon, not in the least nervous at the prospect of facing a wider and more discriminating audience. She had no conceit in her, but she knew she was good. Ivy Rogers had said so, and Alice's customers had confirmed it.

"Mr. Finn, how wonderful! When will it be?"

"To-morrow night. No sense in delaying matters, and it'll give you less time to get jumpy. Don't you agree, Alice?"

Mrs. Dabbs and Herbert were now on first-name terms, he totally smitten and she as skittish as a girl because of his none too subtle courting.

"Opal hasn't a nerve in her body," said Alice proudly, as if she alone were responsible for the fact. "How do you feel about it, Susie? You don't look best pleased."

Susie was standing close to Johnny Dibell so that they could hold hands behind their backs. Like Alice and Herbert, they had wasted no time in admitting how they felt about each other.

"I'm very pleased." Susie flushed with embarrassment. "I didn't mean to seem ungrateful. It's just that I hoped you'd let Johnny come, too."

Finn had already made his assessment of Dibell. A born loser, if ever he'd seen one, but he was soft-hearted like Alice.

"All right, if it's going to cheer you up, Susie. But see here, young man. You can have a chance, but only one. If you can't make 'em laugh in the first minute you've no place in my music hall."

Susie kissed Finn's cheek, her smile restored, but Alice and Opal were quiet. Johnny wasn't going to make it and they knew it. Dibell knew it, too. He'd polish up his jokes that night and try to stop his stomach churning over and over, but it wouldn't be any good. Nothing he had ever done had turned out well, and this wouldn't be any different.

"Thank you sir," he said, trying to sound confident. "I'll have them rolling in the aisles for you."

"Of course you will." Susie could read Johnny's thoughts as if they were her own, swift to prop up his sagging spirits. "He'll do fine, won't he, Opal?"

Opal didn't want to discourage her friend, or make things worse for Dibell, but she wasn't going to raise false hopes either.

"I'm sure he'll do his best, and now we'd better see what costumes we're going to wear. Dear Mr. Finn, I'm so grateful to you. Do you know, you've just made my second-best dream come true."

* * *

Finn's Music Hall was packed on the following evening. In the dressing-room Opal put on her make-up and then got into her costume. She had long ago abandoned playing the little girl. Now she wore a parlour-maid's outfit, with a frilled cap on her head, a crisp white apron and a black dress with a full skirt no longer than her knees. She carried a feather duster as her prop, and her songs recited the trials of one in service, with the master of the house and his grown-up sons forever pursuing their innocent victim.

Alice's friend in the business had written special numbers for Opal, spicing them with wit, double entendres and downright salaciousness. But in spite of the new rôle and the more wicked words, there remained the same innocence about Opal. Her lyrics may have been unchaste, but the image she projected wasn't.

Susie clung to her beggar-child act, for that was the only one she could manage. It still wrung hearts, and Alice had seen no reason to suggest a change.

Susie was on first. She was trembling in the wings, alternately comforted and bullied by Opal and Alice. In the end she managed to get on the boards and give a creditable performance which won her enough applause to satisfy Finn.

Then it was Opal's turn. She nipped on to the stage, looking over her shoulder in alarm as if someone were chasing her, and in that single second the atmosphere in the hall changed.

Those who patronised Finn's establishment were not only sophisticated; they were masters at sorting out good from bad and mediocrity from brilliance. Opal's beauty alone would have got her a hearing, but she had never relied on her appearance. She hardly thought about her looks; it was what she could do which mattered to her.

She saw the sea of faces, a great mass of critics waiting to judge her, and she took them on without a moment's hesitation. These were the people she'd been waiting for. She wasn't simply going to please them; she was going to make them her slaves.

Then she forgot about them as Mrs. Rogers had once told her to do. 'Pretend you're alone,' Ivy had said, and Opal did just that, throwing her heart and soul into her act.

She flipped up her brief skirt, the only part of the old routine she had retained, and it was over. The music died away, and for a moment *Finn's* was as quiet as a grave, the spectators dumb.

Then the roar began. They clapped, they cheered, they stamped their feet and stood up to shout their approval. The noise went on and on, and at the side of the stage Alice buried her head against Herbert's shoulder and wept.

Finn was torn between satisfaction at his own percipience and the effort of swallowing the lump which had suddenly come into his throat.

"Oh, Herbert, she'd done it," whispered Alice, mopping her eyes. "My girl's done it."

"Indeed she has." Finn took the opportunity of giving Alice a hug, surreptitiously reaching for his handkerchief at the same time. "Listen to 'em. They won't let her go."

And they wouldn't. Opal curtsied again and again, but when she tried to make for the wings she was stopped by a fresh howl and a demand for more.

She was quite calm about the effect she had had. She was delighted that she had won the audience over, but she'd never had much doubt that she could do it. She wished Edward could have been there to see her; it would have made her happiness complete.

She had to do two encores before finally she was allowed to slip away into the exultant arms of Alice, Herbert and Susie.

"You've seen the last of Whitechapel," said Finn, pulling

himself together. "You're on to-morrow night and every night after that."

"Oh is she, Herbert Finn? And what about me?"

Herbert winked at Alice.

"I've thought about you, m'dear. Fact is, I never stop thinking about you. I've got an idea I think you'll like. We'll talk about it later."

Alice's protest, a weak one in any event, died away as Finn took her hand and squeezed it. There was no time for further chat for Johnny Dibell was on.

As usual, Dibell's luck was bad. He had to follow a new-born star, and even if he'd been the funniest man alive his task would have been a difficult one.

But he wasn't funny. There wasn't a vestige of humour or talent in him, and after two dreadful minutes the incensed cash-customers booed him off the stage.

In his cupboard-like dressing-room Susie comforted him.

"Dearest, it doesn't matter. They're absolute brutes out there and you mustn't let them upset you."

"I'm no good. I've never been any good."

"Not as a comedian, perhaps, but there are other things to do in the world."

"Not for me."

"Of course for you. Johnny, do you love me?"

He raised his head, and Susie saw the tears on his cheeks. She wanted to cuddle him like a baby, soothing him as a mother would soothe a child who had been hurt. But Johnny was a man, and she knew she mustn't sap any more of his pride.

"You know I do."

"And I love you, so very much. We'll get married as soon as we've saved up a bit."

"I can't let you shackle yourself to a failure like me."

"Don't talk like that; I won't let you. You're not a failure and I'll prove it to you. We'll find you a different kind of job, and soon you'll be earning so much we can buy a mansion to live in."

Dibell took Susie's face between his hands, not ashamed of his grief which he wouldn't have let anyone but her see. She was the embodiment of sweetness and she filled his heart with a deep, radiant warmth. He knew she was wrong about his future, but he wasn't going to dampen her enthusiasm. If she could face that night's disaster, so could he.

"Perhaps even a palace. God I do want you. Will you really marry me?"

"I'm quite set on it." Her own tears weren't far away. There would never be a palace or a mansion for them, but it wasn't important. As long as they could be together nothing else mattered very much. "Get changed now, dear. Mr. Finn and Alice are taking us out to dinner."

"I'd rather go home and have a bite to eat with you."

Susie understood. Johnny was shattered by his experience; the aftermath of Opal's triumph would be more than he could bear.

"Then that's what we'll do, and afterwards – "

He nodded.

"Afterwards I'll tell you again what you mean to me. Susie, you won't ever leave me, will you?"

Susie's gentle laugh was a cure for all ills.

"No, I'll never leave you. How could I? Didn't you know, Johnny Dibell, you're my life? I'm going to be with you for ever and a day."

* * *

A week after Opal's debut, Davey Campbell paid a visit to *Finn's Music Hall*.

He had intended to spend the evening at home, but as he walked up High Holborn he caught sight of a playbill which stopped him in his tracks. There couldn't be two Opal Shannons who had wanted to go on the halls. It had to be his friend from the Lockgate days; the girl who had withstood The Death Hole with such aplomb.

Later that night, as he took his seat, he felt an odd elation. He hadn't had time to make further enquiries as to the whereabouts of Opal after all. The second shop had been followed by a third, then a fourth and fifth. Now he had a dozen stores, six market stalls, and was the owner of thirty ramshackle houses which he let out in rooms at criminally high rents.

He had gone from strength to strength since the day he had first pushed Phineas Weech's barrow. He hadn't always been honest and scrupulous in his dealings, but he had worked like a galley-slave and none of his ventures had ever failed. Money seemed to stick to his fingers, and only twelve months ago he had started investing on the Stock Exchange.

He met a different class of people there and had risen to the challenge of becoming one of them. He had changed his tailor and the kind of mistresses he kept. He left the house in Balham and moved into a larger one in Kensington. He had taken on better-trained staff who understood how to treat the gentry, and had begun to entertain.

Long before he entered the City he had corrected the way he spoke and had gone to fashionable restaurants to watch the table manners of those dining there. It was almost as though he had known what was in store for him and had started to prepare himself for a new life.

No one in his present circle realised that he was a tradesman and a slum landlord. Everyone thought he was just a shrewd investor who gave sound financial tips and excellent supper parties.

He sat patiently through the tumblers, jugglers, a black-robed magician with a wand and a troupe of dancers. Then came a comedian and a bass singer whose notes seemed to come from underneath his feet.

When Opal tripped on to the stage the hall erupted with the sound of cheers and clapping, and Davey smiled. She had always said she would get to the top, and, judging by the audience, she was well on her way.

He listened to her, his pleasure increasing, his applause

louder than anybody's when she had finished. She had indeed made good and had grown even lovelier than he had expected. He made up his mind there and then to make her his mistress. He would buy her a luxurious nest anywhere she wanted it and shower her with jewels, furs, and perfume. He doubted whether she was still a virgin, bearing in mind her line of work, but he didn't really care about that. She'd probably had to use her body to get as far as *Finn's Music Hall*. In her position he would have done the same thing.

When Opal saw Campbell as she came out of her dressing-room she could hardly believe her eyes.

"Davey! I must be dreaming. Is it really you? Did you see my act? What did you think of it?"

"It's me, I did see you, and you were wonderful. Here, give me a kiss."

Davey put his arms round Opal and hugged her. She had expected a salutation on the cheek, but she found his lips against hers and the kiss far from a brotherly one. She told herself not to be so touchy. Just because she had seen Edward the day before and spent an hour in heaven she shouldn't begrudge an old friend a token of affection.

It was later, when Campbell took her to supper, that she knew her fears were correct. Davey was looking at her in a way which even a fool couldn't misunderstand, and his tone was making suggestions not formed into words.

She side-tracked him by telling him about Susie, in bed that evening with a bad cold.

"She sings very well," said Opal when the waiter had served the entrée and moved away. "You must come and see her soon. She's fallen in love, by the way."

"Is he good enough for her?"

"If you mean is he rich, no, but they are devoted to each other. You look prosperous. Tell me about yourself."

Davey knew what Opal was doing, laughing to himself. She was keeping him at arm's length by filling every second with conversation. He'd give her her head for a while; there was no need to hurry. It was the same in business. Often one had to wait for the best things, and he obliged with an expurgated history of his past few years.

"You've done so well. I'm glad for you. Are you married?"

"Do I look it?"

"I'm not sure how a married man looks."

"I'm quite certain that you do, but no, I haven't got a wife. And you? Have you got a compliant husband tucked away somewhere?"

Campbell watched the expression on Opal's face change. She was no longer on the defensive, nor even thinking about him and his overtures. As a womaniser he understood the opposite sex very well. and read her sadness accurately.

"I see. No husband, but there's a man, isn't there?"

"That's enough about me. Tell me more about your investments."

"I doubt if you know what an investment is. What's he like, this chap of yours? Generous, I hope. And is it serious?"

"Davey, I can't talk to you if you're going to treat me like one of your whores."

He was silent for a moment or two, and when he spoke again the hunter in him was dead. This was skinny little Opal Shannon whom he'd rescued from rape, protected against the workhouse bullies, and of whom he was very fond. They hadn't seen each other for years, but the ties which bound them were as secure as ever.

"I'm sorry," he said gently. "Let's begin again. I'm Davey Campbell who gave you a stale crust when you came out of the morgue, remember?"

She gave him a grateful smile, knowing she would have no further trouble with him.

"I'll never forget it."

"We told each other everything in those days. I haven't really changed. I'm still a good listener."

"I'm sure you are, but I can't speak of him, not even to you."

"Then he's not just a wealthy merchant with wandering hands, like me?"

"No, he's not like you. Please – "

"All right, I'm not going to pry. But I must say this, because I care about you. I suspect your lover comes from exalted circles. Don't let him hurt you."

"He won't be able to avoid it, but he'll be hurt, too. I could have refused him, but I didn't. Anything which happens to me is more my fault than his, but thank you for wanting to look after me as you used to in the House. Now may we talk of something else?"

"Yes, the subject's closed. But if ever you're in trouble come to me."

"I promise." She gave a faint laugh. "My last promise was to you. I said I'd help you any time in the future when you were in trouble. I gave my oath on it when you stopped that hateful boy from tearing my dress off. I expect you've forgotten."

"No I haven't, but I believe your need for aid is going to be greater than mine. Will Susie be back soon?"

"To-morrow, probably. Don't leave your next visit too long. Susie speaks of you so often."

"I'll come, if you'll let me take you out to supper again, and it won't be like to-night. I shall bore you silly with a lecture on stocks and shares. Is it a bargain?"

She nodded, wondering why she wanted to cry.

"It's a bargain. Oh, Davey, Davey, it's so very good to have my dear friend back again. I hadn't realised until now how much I've missed you."

Seven

While Edward was in Wiltshire attending to estate business, Gillian made sure she wasn't bored. Having put her mother in her place, she went where she pleased accompanied by Jessie Bolt, her maid and confidante.

One evening she visited her aunt, Lady Naomi Viner, and her cousins, Peter, Geoffrey, Celeste and Alexandra. She found them making preparations to visit *Finn's Music Hall* to see an illusionist about whom they'd heard many spine-chilling reports.

Lady Viner considered Peter, a level-headed twenty-five, sufficient safeguard of the girls' reputation and virtue, and having decided to eat later all but Naomi set out for Holborn.

Gillian wasn't impressed by the various acts which Herbert had engaged, remarking to Celeste the girl in the maid's costume was positively vulgar. Her irritation increased by Peter's view that the singer was ravishing. She didn't like references to other women's good looks, even from her cousin.

It was Alexandra who insisted on going backstage afterwards. She wanted to meet The Great Nabob, who had produced a 'ghost' on stage which had rattled chains and moaned to the accompaniment of weird music.

Alexandra's folly in seeking out the theatrical nobody was, as Gillian realised later, the turning-point in her own life. She barely glanced at The Great Nabob, ignored the dancers and conjurer, and gave the girl with the golden hair and feather duster a very frosty look.

Then she saw the man talking to the girl, and her heart quickened. He was tall, with broad shoulders, hair the colour of copper, and grey eyes. Under the expensive dress-coat with its low velvet-faced collar and the well-cut trousers tapering towards the ankle, there lurked an animal of the kind which filled her mind with carnal longings. There was latent power in him; she could sense it although they were several feet apart.

As Opal went off to dress, Davey Campbell caught Gillian's eye. He felt shock run through him as if he had been hit by a tidal wave. He knew at once that he had never met a woman like this before and never would again.

He had neither expected nor wished to have a serious relationship with a member of the opposite sex, content with his mistresses whom he could pay off when he wearied of them. Now he knew he was no more immune from love than any other man, for in that brief second or two he had lost his heart.

Both Gillian and Davey felt the same sense of being drawn together by a magnetism neither understood. They knew they couldn't leave things as they were. It would be like turning one's back on life itself.

Gillian's cousins were chatting to Finn and the performers and didn't notice Campbell moving towards her. There was too much noise for any of them to hear as Davey said slowly:

"I'm Davey Campbell. What's your name?"

Gillian realised instantly that Campbell had come from humbler beginnings than her own, but it didn't alter her feelings one whit. He was a richer, more polished version of Beamish. In bed he would be just as rough and violent as the coachman would have been, yet there was more to the newcomer than that.

"I'm Gillian Wintour."

"You're the most beautiful creature I've ever seen. I shan't rest until I'm your lover."

She made no pretence at being shocked.

"You don't believe in preliminaries, Mr. Campbell, do you?"

"No, they're a waste of time. You want me as much as I want you."

"How do you know that?"

"I know; so do you. Soon you'll belong to me."

"I'm afraid you're going to be disappointed. I'm engaged to the Earl of Kynston."

"That makes no difference. I'm not asking you to marry me."

"I'm glad to hear it; the answer would be no."

"I don't doubt it. Where do you live?"

"I think it might be unwise to tell you."

As she took a step nearer to him, Davey could smell her perfume and the more subtle fragrance of womanhood.

"Unwise or not, where..."

"Latimer Street."

"Which number?"

"Seven."

"Which is your bedroom?"

Gillian felt a delicious sensation, as if Campbell were stroking her bare flesh.

"Good heavens! Are you going to climb through my window?"

"If we can't find a better way, yes."

"It's on the second floor in the front, but I think a forced entry would be unwise."

"Then I shall stand in the street below and watch the window."

"You're the strangest man I've ever met."

"But the one you'll never forget. I shall send you notes and other things until I can make arrangements for us to be alone. Do you live with your parents?"

"Just my mother. I'm not sure that I want your notes."

"You know perfectly well that you do. You'll want the gifts I send with them because you're acquisitive, like me. Is your mother a problem? Will she ask questions?"

"She knows better than to do that."

"Good. I have to go for I'm taking someone to supper. She's coming now and it would be better if she didn't see us together."

Gillian looked past his shoulder to Opal.

"Oh, that girl who did the maid's number. Is she your mistress?"

"No, just an old friend. Pull your curtains back late to-night."

"I'll do no such thing."

Gillian's voice said one thing, her eyes something quite different.

"You will. Good-night, Miss Wintour. Did anyone ever tell you that your body is magnificent?"

Gillian didn't know how she got through the rest of that evening. She hardly heard the remarks her cousins addressed to her, and they teased her, saying she was dreaming of Edward Adare.

She wondered what they would say if she blurted out that Kynston meant nothing to her, but that one day she would go to bed with a man she had seen for only five minutes, but who had changed the whole world for her.

At twelve o'clock she dismissed her maid. When she was certain that everyone was asleep, she went to the window and drew back the curtains a fraction. By the light of the moon she could see Campbell on the opposite pavement, looking up. She felt hot, as if she had a fever, and the itch in her was almost too strong to bear. She wanted to call out to him to come to her, but that wasn't the way to deal with this particular fish.

He had to be dangled on a string for a while as she played the remote goddess. He had to send the presents he'd promised, and be driven half out of his mind because of his longing for her. Only then would he give her total satisfaction.

Her tongue moistened her lips as she flung the curtains

right back and lit two lamps near the window. Then slowly and with feline grace she began to undress. She knew he wouldn't miss a single move she made and that he would be as aroused as she was at that moment. For a full minute she stood naked, the Nottingham lace curtain draped over her arm so that it shouldn't obstruct his view. Then she was gone, the curtains closed again as she fell on her bed and started to smile.

Campbell knew that he ought to have laughed at her antics, but he couldn't. Already she meant too much to him. His private, inner self had been invaded, and he was vulnerable, a state of things he had never experienced before.

If the gods had asked him to choose between all that he had worked so tirelessly to attain and the girl in the window, he would have chosen the latter. He hungered for her as he had once hungered for food, but the craving now was deeper and much more dangerous.

He turned the corner and got into his carriage, his face sombre.

"Damn you, Gillian Wintour," he said very quietly after he had ordered the driver to take him home. "One day you're going to destroy me and I know it. Christ! Why, of all women, did I have to fall in love with you?"

* * *

The house in Belmer Street which Edward had purchased for Opal made her gasp.

It had none of the flamboyance of *The Canterbury Hall*, which had impressed her so when she was younger. It was furnished with impeccable taste, and although she had never seen anything like it before she knew a small fortune had been spent on it.

She walked from room to room with the earl, her pleasure lighting up her face.

"It's quite splendid," she said when they reached the last closed door. "Edward, I don't know what to say."

"Then say nothing and come and look at the most important part of our domain."

As Opal went into the bedroom she felt the first quiver of apprehension. Kynston had avoided the obvious pink, and chosen oyster satin for the curtains and embroidered bedspread, delicate eighteenth-century furniture and an Aubusson carpet as thick as a snowdrift.

He had lit it with candles which painted shadows in the corners and made small mysteries of everyday objects. After that night's performance Opal had told Alice that she wouldn't be home until very late. Mrs. Dabbs had said nothing, but Opal had seen the doubt in her. She had thought about concocting a story of some sort, but that would be lying. She had never lied to Alice before and she wasn't going to start now.

Her new-found fame had made her more money, and she had spent quite a lot on her wardrobe so that she could live up to Edward's sartorial perfection. She wore a paletot of velvet trimmed with Spanish lace over a matching gown of honey-coloured silk.

As the earl helped her to remove the cape he touched her hair with his lips.

"I don't want to stop here, sweetheart," he said softly. "I want to undress you. Do you mind?"

Opal couldn't help the faint blush in spite of her yearning for Edward. It was why they had come to the house, to the bedroom yet she was a virgin and feared she might not measure up to Kynston's expectations.

He seemed to read her thoughts and put a tender hand on her cheek.

"I know this is the first time for you, but you don't have to be afraid."

She gave him a doubtful smile, glad when his fingers closed over hers in comfort.

"I know that. I'm not frightened of you because I feel I know you as well as I know myself. I just don't want to disappoint you. As you say, I've had no experience and – "

He laughed, the sound like a caress.

"If you had, you wouldn't be here now. Come, let me shew you what love really means."

It was clear to Opal that if she was a novice, Edward wasn't. He disrobed her slowly, making the removal of each garment an erotic gesture. She had realised that he would have had mistresses and didn't think the worse of him for that. He was so handsome that many women must have wanted him as she wanted him now.

At the first touch of his hand she was filled with trembling excitement. His fingers made her body feel like silk, soft and seductive. Her breath quickened as he explored the contours of her thighs and breasts, her nipples hardening in desire.

All her doubts were gone. In their place was a sudden, overpowering longing to know Edward's real strength, and she pressed closer to him, her own hands searching as eagerly as his.

The earl understood, responding at once. As he covered her body with his own he was no longer gentle, and the hunger in her was rabid. In the place where her innocence had dwelt undisturbed she felt a strange, unrecognisable sensation. It began as lightly as the tickle of a feather, rising to a crescendo which made her writhe under him. She was like a wild creature, growing more frenzied by the second, gasping aloud as the magic swamped her senses.

Time and place were forgotten as she forced him on and on, begging him to end her torment. His final demand had cruelty in it, yet it was nothing like the description of sexual intercourse given by the women in Lockgate. They had made the moment of penetration seem a sullied, ugly thing, giving pleasure only to the man.

To Opal it was the triumphant climax of a passion shared. It was joy, because she now belonged to Edward completely. It was satisfaction, because her orgasm had richly fulfilled a deep primitive need in her. It was relief, because she hadn't failed him after all.

And now she had learned the true lesson of love. It wasn't merely the exchange of kisses and terms of endearment. It was the miracle of Edward's manhood inside her, her whole being engulfed in an inexplicable fire. Their union had been as perfect as any two mortals could make it, and she lay back with a sigh.

For a moment or two they lay side by side saying nothing. Words would have spoiled the moment, and they were content to wait for exhaustion to pass and for the real world to creep into the bedroom again.

Finally the earl propped himself up on one elbow and twisted a strand of her hair round his finger.

"No woman has ever made me feel as I do now. You're a witch, and I love you."

She smiled, savouring her joy.

"I love you, too. I had no idea I would enjoy it so. Am I a wanton, do you think?"

"Beyond a doubt, praise be to God."

"I suppose I'm a whore now."

"Oh, my darling, don't think of yourself like that."

She reached up to kiss him.

"I like being a whore; your whore. It wasn't a complaint. When can we be together again?"

"Next week."

"So long?"

"I know, but – "

She put her finger over his lips to silence him.

"I'm teasing you. I know how difficult our situation is and all the other things you have to do. Besides, I shall have six whole days to dream about being in your arms again. Edward, when we – that is – when it's over, you will remember me, won't you? Not always, of course, I wouldn't expect that. Just now and again, when you have a minute to spare, think of this night and how wonderful it was."

She saw the sadness in him and watched his smile fade as he spoke.

"If only I could put you into a recess of my mind and just

bring you out at convenient moments it wouldn't be so bad. As it is, I shall see your face wherever I look, hear your voice, feel your closeness, and hunger for your body all of my days."

"I know, I know. It will be just the same for me. I'm sorry. I promised we wouldn't talk of the future, and now I've made you unhappy. Don't look like that, Edward, or I shall cry. Think of next Thursday and kiss me. Oh, Edward, kiss me!"

He drew her into his arms, the pain hidden as their mouths met to give and receive both solace and ecstasy. Neither were aware that a draught had blown the candles out, leaving them in a world of warmth and darkness.

They were in love, and nothing else mattered.

* * *

It was no surprise to Johnny Dibell to discover that the lowest form of music hall manager had no time for him. Even the owners of the penny gaffs spared him no more than a few minutes before turning him away with scorn.

He continued to do odd jobs for Alice Dabbs and sleep in her cellar, spending every spare moment he could find with Susie. He had taken to drinking in a run-down pub a few streets away. *The Golden Crown* served second-rate beer to third-rate human beings, but at least Johnny didn't feel so out of place there. He was just another bit of dross which had washed up against the dirty bar, lacking money and hope.

One day a more prosperous-looking man came to stand by Dibell as he ordered a tankard of ale.

The man, Joseph Webb, was disposed to be friendly, commenting on the dire surroundings and saying that he would never have entered such a hole had his thirst not become too raging to be endured.

Webb told Johnny of his small theatre in the Mile End

Road and how successful it was becoming. Then he gave Dibell another, keener glance.

"Down on your luck?"

"Completely. I can't get work no matter how hard I try."

"Never give up; that's my motto. What d'yer do?"

Dibell explained, and Webb pursed his lips.

"Mm, can't help you there, I'm afraid. Mine's not a music hall and we've no use for comedians, except – "

Johnny felt his throat constrict.

"Yes?"

"We're putting on a comedy next week. Caste's complete, 'cept for someone to play the village idiot. The audience love the simple-minded; makes 'em feel superior. What about it?"

Dibell was screaming inside. He had failed in his own sphere and that was bad enough. Being the butt of the rest of Webb's players and the public was something else. Then he forced himself to be sensible, crushing down his impotent anger so it shouldn't spoil his chance of making a few shillings.

"I've never done straight acting before. What would I have to do?"

"Experience don't matter, not for this job. Just roll your eyes, slobber a bit, fall over as often as you can, and don't hit back when you get knocked about."

Dibell closed his eyes. He was debased and sick at heart, but he couldn't sponge on Alice and Susie for ever. When he had been told what the pay would be he nodded. It wasn't much, but it was better than having to take Susie's coppers when he wanted a drink.

After details were settled he went back to tell Susie. She saw his face and wanted to weep. He looked so defeated and sad, as if the end of the world had come.

"And so I'm to be the buffoon," he said after she had given him something to eat. "Roll my eyes, Webb said, and fall about. Take plenty of knocks, but never hit back. Susie, I'm sorry. I'm such a damned failure."

She held him in her arms, murmuring softly to ease his despair.

"Don't say that of yourself. You haven't failed. You've got a part in a play and someone has to take on the rôle. You could make something of it if you tried. It's a chance to shew how funny you can be."

"As a loony?"

"Why not? Mr. Webb said the audience loved whoever played the village idiot, so you'll have all the people on your side. You don't have to hate what you're doing. Enjoy it; make it fun. Once you can make everyone laugh, you've won."

"Dear Susie, how sweet you are. Only you could pretend that degradation was really success in disguise."

"I mean it. Stop thinking of it in that way. You're a comedian, so make them laugh. What does it matter how you do it? Everyone's sad or worried or frightened. Just for a while, make them forget their troubles."

"All right, I'll try. I've accepted Webb's offer anyway. It's all my fault, thinking I could be a funny man. As I told you, when my brothers and sisters were young I was the one who made them laugh. We used to have pantomimes every Christmas, and even my sour old Aunt Minnie chuckled at me. That's why I thought I could make a living as a comic, but no one's even smiled at my jokes since I left home."

"Well, they will in time. I shall come and see you as soon as I can get an evening off."

"No." He was sharp. "I don't want you to see me making a fool of myself."

"Johnny!"

He saw her indignation and gave in.

"Sorry. Come whenever you like and watch me make them hold their sides. Dearest, what should I do without you?"

"I've told you plenty of times before that you don't have to be without me. I'll always be here for you."

She drew back, and he saw the colour in her cheeks deepen.

"Susie? What is it?"

"You may think it terrible of me to suggest this, but I'm only doing it because we need each other to keep going."

"Suggest what?"

"Well, that we – that you and I should – "

He was still gazing at her, not understanding what she was trying to say and she gave him an impatient shake.

"Goodness me, Johnny Dibell, you are an idiot and no mistake. I want to come down to the cellar to-night when everyone's asleep so that we can make love."

For a while he said nothing, then he took her hand in his.

"I've never wanted any woman but you, and I'll never forget what you've just offered me, but the answer is no. I'm going to marry you before I take any liberties, and that's final."

Susie's eyes filled with tears.

"I think I knew you'd say that, and in a way I'm glad you did. It shews how much you care for me, and I feel as if someone's just given me a precious gem."

"Nothing I could give you would be precious. More like paste."

"If I say it's precious then it is. Now, enough of your moping, my lad. You've got a future now, whether you can see it or not, so how about another cup of tea to celebrate?"

* * *

"Annie, you can't go to Florence on your own. I shall come with you."

"Indeed you won't. Whicker will accompany me, and the villa has enough servants to look after a regiment."

Edward was worried. Annice was wearing her pig-headed expression. Once she had made up her mind to do something it was almost impossible to stop her, but he had to try. She was old, and travelling was tiring. An uncomfortable doubt was niggling at him. She seemed paler than usual; small and frail, only her determination keeping her backbone straight.

"Is there some special reason why you have to go just now?"

Annice lied soothly, like a well-rehearsed actress. The physician hadn't wrapped up his diagnosis; he knew the duchess too well for that. In any case he suspected she had already guessed the truth, and when he spoke of the cancer eating her up inside she had merely inclined her head shewing no emotion.

"No, it's simply that I want to see Florence again before I get too decrepit to make the journey. The villa gardens are beautiful at this time of year. Why shouldn't I go and stay there for a while?"

"No reason, I suppose, but I could – "

"Edward, I don't want you tagging at my heels. I know you're thinking of my welfare and I'm grateful, but I'm going to keep my independence as long as I can. Besides, surely you don't want to leave London just at the moment, do you?"

The earl pulled a face. As he had told Opal, it was virtually impossible to conceal anything from his grandmother, and her tone left no doubt that she was aware of his *affaire*.

"You know about Opal and me?"

"Naturally. Did you really imagine I would remain in ignorance?"

"No, I told Opal you'd find out, though heavens knows how you did so."

"From a very discreet source; you've nothing to worry about."

"Does it shock you – what we are doing?"

The duchess clenched her teeth for a second until the violence of a stab of pain subsided. Then she gave a derisive cackle.

"Shock me? Be your age, Kynston."

"Well, are you angry about it?"

"Not in the least." The spasm seemed to have gone, but Annice knew another would soon take its place and she had to get rid of Edward quickly. "I expect I'd have done the same if I'd had the chance. You've only a few months, my dear. Make the most of them and stop bothering your head about me. I'm quite all right; I simply want to take a short holiday."

"If you're sure." Kynston was still uneasy. Something about their conversation wasn't quite right, but he couldn't put his finger on it. "I would rather stay here if I can. Opal and I haven't got long together, as you say."

"Quite. Has the date of the wedding with that hussy been fixed yet?"

"No, Gillian seems in no hurry, and I – well, neither am I."

"You'll have to make the arrangements soon. You can't drift on indefinitely. And if Gillian Wintour isn't pressing you to name the day, you may be certain she's up to something."

"What sort of something? Have you heard gossip about her?"

"Not yet." Her Grace was put out. "Nevertheless, I know her kind. Really, Edward, you were a cretin to offer for her."

"So you said before, but even if I hadn't done so I couldn't have married Opal. These few months are all we're going to have. They're very precious, Annie."

The duchess laid a gnarled hand on her grandson's cheek.

"I understand, my dear, only too well."

"And you can manage without me?"

The pain was coming back, stronger and with more savagery.

"I can manage a great deal better without you fussing round me. Now go away, I've got things to do. And don't waste a single second of your happiness. It'll be the last you'll have this side of heaven."

When the earl had gone, Annice closed her eyes. She was trying to fight an enemy, knowing she had no chance of victory.

"Your Grace?"

Annice looked up at the concern on Doris Whicker's face. She hadn't been able to hide her secret from Doris, and the latter had proved much more of a source of strength than the duchess had ever thought possible.

"I need a draught – one of those noxious powders Dr. Bellinger left for me. And we'd better bring forward our departure date. I want to leave England before Edward guesses the truth. He gave me an odd look or two just now, and he's nobody's fool."

Doris mixed the powder in a glass of water, feeling pain of her own. Her Grace might be acid at times, but she had never wanted to work for anyone else. Much generosity; so many small kindnesses; such dry humour. And now unbelievable courage in the battle against a slow, dreadful death.

"Don't you think that Master Edward ought to be told?"

"No I don't, and for the ten thousandth time stop calling him Master Edward. Give me that or you'll spill it all over the place."

Once the medicine was down, the duchess looked at Doris's watery eyes.

"Enough of that, you silly goose. We're going to Florence, one of the most beautiful places on earth. You'll enjoy it, even if you can't understand a word that anyone says to you."

Whicker nodded.

"I'm sure I will, but I'd give my own life willingly if I could make you well again."

The duchess smiled.

"I know, though goodness knows why you want to. I'm an irascible old woman, getting more short-tempered by the hour."

Doris blew her nose vigorously.

"Before I knew you were ill I'd never have dared say this to you. Now I'm going to, even if you do bite my head off afterwards. I love you, Your Grace, I really do."

"I know that, too, and I don't deserve it. And you're not the only one who cares. I'm just as fond of you as you are of me. Well, that's enough of maudlin sentiment for today. This medicine leaves a most peculiar taste in my mouth. Go and get a bottle of the best brandy and two glasses. Doris, my girl, you and I are going to get good and tiddly."

Eight

"What is it, Edward? You're so sad."

The earl stirred, his arm tightening round Opal.

"I'm sorry. I hoped you hadn't noticed."

"But I did, and not only this evening. There've been other times recently when I've seen that look on your face. I'm not good for you; I make you unhappy."

"That isn't true." His denial was quick. "Any man lucky enough to be with you should be filled with joy. It's just that – "

"You wish time could stand still."

"Yes I do. I know we agreed we wouldn't talk of the future, but it's difficult not to think about it when it's rushing towards one. I do try to fight my weakness, but then I realise what my life will be like when we have to part. So many years without you; such a long, long time before I die and can escape my misery."

Opal consoled him in the only way she knew how, her mouth against his. She had been increasingly worried by the desolation she had seen growing in Kynston, knowing their liaison was the cause of it. Theirs wasn't a casual *affaire* which Edward could shrug off when he married. Each meeting made the bonds which held them together tighter and more painful. It took all her courage to make the suggestion, but she had to do it because she loved Edward so much.

"Would it be easier if we parted now? If that would help – "

"No!" He dismissed the idea out of hand. "No, I want every minute I can get with you. Forgive me. It's equally bad for you, but you don't complain."

"I do inside." Opal sat up, the candle-light making an alabaster statue of her body. "When I'm alone I cry and rage because life's so unfair. But I wouldn't change a thing if I had to make the decision over again. I'd still want to belong to you if only for a while."

"You're beautiful. Whenever I see candles I shall think of you and how you look at this moment."

"I'll never light another candle as long as I live. I couldn't bear it."

"Oh, my dear!"

They came together desperately, trying to blot out everything but the wonder of being together.

But when Opal left the house in Belmer Street, guilt fell over her once more. She had been selfish to grab the few months with the earl. If she had refused Kynston when they had sat looking at each other across the tea-cups he wouldn't be suffering so much now. At that stage their love had only just started to unfold; ignored, the bud would eventually have withered with the passing of the years. Now they were lovers its roots were deep, its growth invincible. She had thought only of her own longing. She worshipped Edward, but she was tearing him apart by her very existence.

She got into the carriage which...as waiting for her and closed her eyes, the clatter of the wheels over cobblestones drowning her whisper.

"Dear Edward, I shouldn't have let this happen, never, never, never! Oh God, why wasn't I strong enough to say no?"

* * *

Davey Campbell lay back in his chair and gazed round the room which he had prepared for Gillian. For three weeks she had kept him on tenterhooks, acknowledging his notes and expensive trinkets in the most casual of ways.

It hadn't bothered him. Although they had only met once he could see through her like a pane of glass. She had made his loins ache when she had stood naked in the window looking down at him, but she wanted him as much as he needed her.

He had told her in his letters that he was in love with her. At first, he had had some hesitation in putting such a weapon into her hands. In the end, he had thrown caution to the four winds for he had to make her see what she really meant to him. She had ignored his ardour, as she had ignored his pleas that they should become lovers. It was just another move in the dance she was leading him.

But two days ago her response had been different. It had been delivered by Jessie, whom Gillian assured him they could trust. The maid waited as he read it, eyeing him knowingly.

'I shall tell my mother that I'm spending Friday night with friends,' Gillian had written. 'Rent a house, but not some hole in the corner. I want the air to be full of perfume, with flowers all around me, and satin sheets on the bed. There'll also have to be somewhere for Bolt to sleep. If you can manage all that in forty-eight hours I shall know you are serious in what you say and perhaps I'll go to bed with you. On Friday morning I'll send for the address, if there is one.'

It had been another piece of mischief, giving him an almost impossible deadline, and Davey knew that she would have been smiling to herself as she dictated her terms.

The challenge was one he met without hesitation. He found a small place in a quiet part of Belgravia and bought the furnishings for the bed himself, ordering masses of flowers to be delivered early on Friday. He purchased the most expensive scent he could find and went to Bond Street to choose a pair of diamond earrings.

It was nearly nine o'clock by the time he had finished his survey of the bedroom. Even the most demanding of women would be hard put to it to find fault with it, but then Gillian wasn't like other women.

She would be late, of course. She'd leave him in suspense for as long as possible, hoping he would roast on a rack of self-doubt and despair.

Her tardiness gave him time to reflect on his feelings for Gillian and hers for him. The latter were easy enough to assess. She was hot for what he could give her in bed, for she was a marvellous female animal with a strong sexual urge. He had realised that when they had first met, and the well-born, disdainful Miss Wintour would change like a chameleon between the sheets. When it was over she would forget all about it. To her, it would be just a matter of assuaging an appetite like any other.

It was his own feelings which were so hard to come to terms with. She had got into his blood on that first evening at the music hall and he knew it was a disease from which he would never recover. He thought about her constantly, wanting to be with her, longing to protect and cherish her for all her days. He had harsh thoughts about Kynston because the latter would have that privilege, while he, Davey, would never be more than a shadowy figure on the fringe of her life.

The small inner voice which had warned him that she would destroy him was louder than ever, but he pretended not to hear it. His sense of doom had grown stronger each time he received her missives, as if they were stepping-stones to hell. She didn't want him simply to cure the lust in her. She was hoping to break him into pieces like a destructive child tugging off the arms and legs of a doll.

Yet although he could see his descent into the pit so clearly, he couldn't push her away. He adored her with a fierce passion which subdued common sense and left his iron will like a piece of limp string. Just knowing that she existed made each new morning an excitement to him. She was his whole life, and he had no doubt that one day she would be his death.

When she finally arrived his heart almost stopped beating. She wore white satin, like a bride, and he knew she had chosen the gown with malicious care. It was another dig at him, reminding him that she was to be another man's wife. He accepted it as he accepted all the small injuries she had inflicted upon her in her letters. She was exquisite and virginal, until one looked into her eyes, and he began to sweat as she spoke.

"Well, Mr. Campbell, I see you've fulfilled my first requirements. Now let's see what you can do about the rest. I want a master." Her voice was hard, giving him no quarter. "I don't care how much you hurt me, but if you disappoint me you'll never see me again."

"I shan't disappoint you. There's no gentleness in me where you're concerned. Are you sure you know what you're asking for?"

"Quite sure."

"Then get undressed."

"I'll undress when I'm ready." She challenged him from the start, seeing what he would make of her resistance. "Don't give me orders, you peasant."

Even as she insulted him, Gillian hoped he would pass the test with flying colours. She needed a man, a man as rough and brutal as she knew Campbell could be. She had been delighted when he had offered her his heart. It gave her a heady sense of power, yet now she wanted him to bend her to his will. If he couldn't get the better of her at this crucial stage of their relationship, he would be no use to her.

Campbell read her message as accurately as he had read all her other manoeuvres. He understood completely what she wanted from him and he intended to give it to her in good measure.

He slapped her face hard, and before she could give vent to her outrage he had picked her up and thrown her across the bed.

Afterwards they drank champagne and ate oysters. Gillian was fingering the diamond earrings which Campbell had given her, utterly contented and relaxed. She doubted if Edward Adare could give her as much pleasure as Davey had done. She would have to make the most of her plebeian lover in the time left to her.

"When can you come again?" Campbell had never felt as he did just then. Gillian's body had set his own on fire, and the embers still burned fiercely. It was as if he had only just started to live properly, all his senses sharpened, his mind alert. She was all he wanted; all he would ever want. "Next Friday?"

"Perhaps." Gillian was teasing him again, secure in the knowledge that he adored her and that she could twist him round her little finger. "I'll have to think about it."

He caught her wrist with steely fingers as he said softly:

"Next Friday, or I'll come and drag you out of your house."

For a split second Gillian saw something in him which frightened her. Then it was gone, and she was in control again.

"All right, next Friday. But do get lilies next time. Roses are so common, aren't they? There's a lot I'll have to teach you, but I don't mind that. I find you quite amusing. Oh, and I'll have rubies next week. They're my favourite stone. You won't forget, will you?"

Campbell regarded her sardonically. She was a greedy, unscrupulous, heartless bitch, but he didn't care. Possessing her had made him feel like a god and had done nothing to quench his intolerable thirst for her. If anything, it had increased it to proportions which made him tremble inside.

He picked up his glass, keeping his tone as cool as hers.

"No, I won't forget. I'll never forget anything you say to me. Don't worry, my dear, I'm very quick to learn. Next time you shall have rubies."

* * *

"My dear, I don't want to upset you but there's something I

think you really ought to know."

The Hon. Dulcie Henneker was slim, soignée and worldly-wise, with hair the colour of a fox's brush and small, alert eyes. She and Gillian had been friends since childhood, sharing a music master, a dancing instructress, and a miserable wan who had tried to teach them to sketch whilst they pulled faces at her and practised cruelty in a way which only the young can do.

Dulcie and Gillian squabbled frequently, criticising each other's clothes, friends and morals, but the tie between them overrode such trivialities. They could be honest with each other, not having to pick and choose their words, and somewhere under the brittle surface of their relationship was a measure of affection which neither of them ever admitted.

Gillian was caustic as she handed Dulcie her cup.

"Of course you want to upset me; you never miss a chance of doing so. What is it this time?"

Dulcie giggled.

"Yes, I suppose I do; we both do, don't we? Well, never mind that. It's about Kynston's latest mistress."

"Is that all? I've always known he's not a monk, but he's a good deal more continent than many men. Besides, it's me he's going to marry."

"I agree, but why should he choose a girl brought up in a workhouse who's now on the music halls? A trifle eccentric, don't you think?"

"Do you know her name?"

Gillian had grown very still, not at all surprised when Dulcie told her it was Opal Shannon. Somehow she had known she would encounter again the girl she'd seen at *Finn's Music Hall*. She had taken an instant dislike to her and now her anger was savage. She didn't let Dulcie see her rage; her friend would have gloated too much. Instead, she listened in silence to the tale of Carter, Dulcie's maid, whose bosom pal, Batsford, was a parlour-maid at the house next door to Edward's love-nest.

"It's the oddest coincidence," said Dulcie, helping herself to a biscuit. "Shannon was in Lockgate Workhouse at the same time as Batsford was there. She remembers her quite well. Even though Shannon was young then, she was a trouble-maker. She and a boy called Davey Campbell were always in hot water. That's why they made such an impression on Batsford."

Gillian's anger began to fade into a kind of satisfaction. She had always made a point of collecting and filing away in the recesses of her mind odd bits of gossip and scandal. She wasn't sure why she did so, save that knowledge was power, and one never knew when one would want a weapon or two to hand.

Now Dulcie had given her something which was really worthwhile storing in her memory. She didn't care a button about Kynston's other peccadilloes, but this was different. One day she'd make him and the Shannon woman pay for their casual pleasure.

The revelation that Campbell had been a pauper boy in a workhouse was even more useful to know about. At present he would have given her the moon had she asked for it, but if there should ever be a reluctance on his part to fall in with her wishes she now had the perfect instrument with which to coerce him.

She saw Dulcie's eager expression and said lightly:

"Really, how absurd of Edward to choose someone like that."

"Quite, but I understand she's very beautiful."

"No doubt."

Dulcie pricked up her ears. There was something in Gillian's voice she'd never heard before and she worried away at the topic like a dog with a bone.

"I suppose you've never seen her?"

Gillian's faint surprise would have put many a professional actress to shame.

"Seen her? A creature from the workhouse. How could I have done so? You're being too ridiculous."

"What are you going to do about it?"

"Nothing. Let Kynston have his fun while he can. He'll meet the bill later, you may be sure of that."

Dulcie nodded.

"Oh, I'm sure. Diamonds, perhaps, and pearls?"

"One or the other. Now do let's change the subject; it's beginning to bore me. Is it true that Mary Tavistock has run away from her husband?"

For a second Dulcie hesitated, but she could see she'd get nothing more out of Gillian just then. She must have imagined what she thought she saw in her friend's eyes. How could Gillian possibly know the earl's paramour?

"Absolutely true." She held out her cup, quite happy to turn to another piece of scandal. "Give me some more tea, dear, and I'll tell you all about it. Really! Some women never know when they're well off."

* * *

When Gillian found that she was pregnant she was panic-stricken. Terror crowded in on her like dark thunder-clouds. She could hear Kynston's voice condemning her as he severed all ties with her; the excited buzz of polite society deafened her.

When her head cleared she began a frantic search for a solution. An abortion was out of the question. When she was seven years old she'd seen one of her mother's maids die in agony as a result of the girl's visit to a woman in a back street. Gillian could still hear the maid's terrible screams and see the blood, remembering how she'd been rooted to the spot until her governess had come and dragged her away. Whatever the answer to her predicament was, Gillian wasn't going to let herself suffer in such a way.

Next, she considered giving the unwanted infant away, but that wouldn't be easy either. She could make an excuse to leave London for a few months when her condition became obvious, but Davey Campbell would raise difficulties about adoption. He had read in a newspaper not long before of a child, not wanted by its mother, who had died as a result of ill-treatment by its foster parents. He had waxed furious, saying that if he had a son or daughter, nothing would induce him to pack it off to strangers as if it were a bundle of rubbish.

It wasn't that Gillian cared a fig about Davey's views on such things. Her only concern was that she needed his help and money to see her through the mess he had helped to create. He would have to be handled very carefully, and she would have to think of someone to take the baby whom Campbell would trust.

Then quite suddenly she saw the answer. Her fear was all for nothing because Dulcie had shewn her the way to deal with the matter with her gossip about Opal Shannon and Campbell spending the early years of their life in a workhouse. Campbell had his reputation to think about; he couldn't afford to let his history be known. Edward's mistress could be forced to help, too. She was said to be an old friend of Davey's, and presumably wouldn't want Edward dragged into a sordid situation either if she truly cared for him.

When she was shewn into Opal's dressing-room that night she started as she meant to go on. The girl must see no weakness in her; she, Gillian, had to be in command from the start.

"Miss Shannon, I'm Gillian Wintour."

Opal turned from the mirror feeling a spasm of dread. Edward had mentioned her visitor's name and said his grandmother didn't approve of his choice, but she had never expected to see his fiancée, least of all at *Finn's*.

The sight of Gillian, beautiful in her gown of rose tulle and heavy satin, left Opal dumbfounded. The woman's face could have been painted by an Italian master, but it was hard and cold as stone. The chill in Opal increased. Something very bad was about to happen and she felt wholly vulnerable before the icy stare.

She was trying to think of some suitable response when Gillian took the conversation in hand.

"In order to save time, Miss Shannon, let me tell you that I know you're Edward's mistress and that you visit him twice a week at a house in Belmer Street."

The colour drained from Opal's cheeks, and it was hard to get words out because her mouth was so dry.

"How did you find out?"

"Does it matter? The point is that I did."

Opal felt as if she was in the middle of a nightmare as she held on to the back of her chair. She sensed that this call wasn't just a warning to her to leave Edward alone. It was something much worse than that, but what the real blow was to be she had no idea.

"You want me to stop seeing the earl, of course."

Gillian gave a brief laugh.

"You'll stop doing that right enough, but I want more from you than that."

"I don't understand."

"Probably not, but I'll explain it very clearly to you. I know that you're a friend of Davey Campbell's and that you were together in Lockgate Workhouse. Davey and I are lovers, and now I'm pregnant by him. It's too tedious for words, but I'm not going to put my life at risk by getting rid of the baby, and Davey will be tiresome about farming the brat out to someone he doesn't know."

Opal was trying to regain her composure, but what Gillian was saying made it almost impossible. Her limbs felt as stiff as wood, her mind fuzzy with shock. And somewhere deep inside herself she had started to mourn because she knew she was going to lose Edward earlier than she had expected.

Gillian ignored the effect she was having, taking a seat opposite Opal.

"If you were to take the baby when it's born, Davey would accept that. As you're such an old friend of his, he'd trust you. It would suit me, too, because I don't want it to go to someone who might find out the truth one day and blackmail me. My future's too important for that. So you see, you're the ideal person."

Opal pulled herself together with an effort.

"If I were to take it? But why should I?"

Gillian's smile was frightening.

"Because if you refuse to do so, I'd tell all Davey Campbell's precious new friends in the City about his background. What do you think they'd say when they heard he was a guttersnipe reared in a workhouse? He'd be finished. He's worked so hard for what he's got; I'll give him that. He will lose it all if I start talking."

"You couldn't do that. You must have some feeling for him."

"Don't be so naïve, and of course I could talk, and will, if I have to. As to Edward, if you've any real love for him you'll want to help him, too. If it was discovered that I was pregnant by Davey he'd be a laughing-stock. Think of the whispers which would go on behind his back. Poor, foolish Edward who'd played second fiddle to a tradesman. Mud would stick to his name and that would upset his old harridan of a grandmother. Still, I don't suppose that interests you very much."

Opal felt waves of sickness wash over her. Gillian Wintour was right. Davey would be ruined if his past was uncovered, and Edward would become a figure of fun. Only in one respect was Miss Wintour wrong. She, Opal, did care about the duchess. It was the latter who had sent her to Alice Dabbs. It was a debt which had to be paid, just like the one she owed Davey who had saved her from rape when she was young.

Gillian was delighted with the way things were going. She had expected a shrill, ranting shrew who would fight her every inch of the way. She hadn't even been certain if the threats would work, but they had, and most satisfactorily. Shannon had no anger in her; just a kind of dumb helplessness which Gillian built on quickly before the girl had time to think straight.

"And you owe me something." Her stare was unwavering. "You became Edward's doxy after I was betrothed to him. I'm entitled to some recompense for that."

Opal continued to sit in silence, and Gillian was tart.

"For heaven's sake say something. Are you going to take the child when it arrives? I've given you good enough reasons why you should. It'll mean you'll have to leave here for a while, but you'll soon find other work when it's over. Your sort always do and no one will think anything about you having an illegitimate baby. When you tell Edward you're Campbell's mistress and are going to have his child he'll be done with you for good. I don't want him mooning over some lost love for the rest of his days."

Finally the full enormity of what was happening struck Opal.

"When I tell Edward?"

"Well, of course you'll have to tell him, won't you? It's part of the price you've got to pay for sleeping with him and for saving your friend Davey."

The room seemed to fade away, and Opal was in Pavini's with Edward, assuring him that she was prepared to settle the account in full for the privilege of loving him for a while. Then Edward was gone again and she was back with her tormentor, knowing she would have to agree to what was demanded of her.

"If I accept," she said wearily, "how can we possibly manage things so that people don't find out the truth?"

"You will accept and the rest is simple enough. We'll let things go on as they are for a while. When I begin to shew we'll go to Norfolk where we have a house. Mother and Jessie, my maid, won't cause any trouble. Mother's terrified of losing Kynston's money and Jessie will do anything I tell her to."

"It will ruin me."

Gillian was curt. The bargain was almost sealed, but she couldn't soften her tone. Victory was within her grasp and she wasn't going to let it slip away.

"You deserve to be ruined. You should have stuck to your own kind and not reached so high for your lover. You've only yourself to thank. I want your promise now, or to-morrow I'll visit a banker in Threadneedle Street whom I know. Well, what's it to be? How much of a friend are you to Campbell and just how much do you love Edward Adare?"

* * *

"A child? Gillian, my dearest, are you sure?"

Gillian stifled the sharp retort which sprang to her lips. She had got Opal's agreement to the plan, but Davey still had to be coaxed into accepting it.

"Of course I am."

"Then we must marry. You'll have to tell Kynston the engagement is off."

"Don't be absurd." The irritation couldn't be avoided that time. "He must never find out about this. I told you from the start that I was going to marry him and why."

Davey felt the delight in him seeping away. His need for Gillian grew day by day, every thought and action of his coloured by his passion. Now his seed was in her womb, but she was still rejecting him.

"For his name, his title, and his fortune, he said dully. "Do those things matter to you so much?"

"They do." Gillian was in control of herself again. "Darling, you know we could never marry. There are too many stumbling-blocks between us. And we're very happy as we are, aren't we?"

In fact, Gillian was getting less and less happy with Campbell's possessiveness and jealousy. At first it had amused her to be worshipped like a goddess. Now she found it as restricting as a prison and wished that she could be free of him.

"I suppose so." Campbell knew he was beaten. Gillian was never going to give up her world for him, and if he wanted to remain her lover he would have to toe the line. "But what about the child? I'm not going to let you give it away to any Tom, Dick or Harry."

"I know, sweet, I know. But I've found the answer to the whole problem. I've made a plan with the help of a friend of yours, Opal Shannon."

Davey felt his nerve-end twitch. Gillian was too self-assured, too pleased with herself.

"Opal? I didn't think you knew her. What's she got to do with this?"

"Everything." Gillian was soothing. "Now come and sit down beside me and I'll tell you all about it."

When she had finished Campbell sat for a while staring down at his clenched hands. He didn't know why he was surprised at the depths to which Gillian was prepared to sink. He had always known she was heartless, caring for no one but herself.

"You're a hard-nosed little bitch, aren't you?" he asked finally, and raised his head to look at her. "You haven't got a grain of compassion in you."

"Perhaps not."

She was unmoved by his censure, sure that he would give way in the end. If he hadn't been prepared to agree he would have stormed out of the room as soon as she had stopped talking.

"No perhaps about it. You're willing to destroy me and Opal just to keep yourself out of trouble and get what you want from Kynston. You can't ask such a thing of Opal."

"Why not? She's Edward's mistress and deserves to pay for that. Besides, she's said she'll do it for your sake. You ought to be thankful that I'm so clever at working things out."

"I want to hear that agreement from her myself."

"If you insist. I'm told she'll be at Belmer Street at seven to-night. That's the house Kynston bought for her, but he's away for a day or two so you'll be quite safe. It seems she can't stay away from the place whether Edward's there or not. Go and see her by all means; it's number twenty-two. And Davey – "

"What?"

"Remember this. If you help me I'll go on being your mistress after I'm married. We can sleep together and have just as much fun. If you refuse I'll be out of your life for good. Could you bear that?"

Campbell knew he ought to tell her to go to hell, but he couldn't do it. It wasn't the thought of the fall from grace in the City which bothered him. It was the frightening knowledge that if he made objections he would never see Gillian again. She had sapped his strength by her witchcraft, draining his manhood from him because he wanted her too much. He didn't even have enough spirit left to challenge her; to ask what she would do if he failed to co-operate and Kynston threw her over when her condition became obvious. He was under her thumb and couldn't fight her.

Gillian saw his weakness, taking his face between her hands. Her eyes shone with false ardour as she delivered the *coup-de-gràce*.

"Could you bear it, Davey, losing my love?"

"You know I couldn't." It sounded like someone else's voice answering her question; an alien sound in his ears. "I don't care about my business; that isn't important. But I can't give you up. Damn you, Gillian, damn you! I'll never give you up."

Nine

"You don't have to go through with this, you know."

Opal and Campbell were in the drawing-room of twenty-two Belmer Street, talking quietly, sharing trouble as they had done years before.

"If I don't she will bring you down, Davey. She has the means and she won't hesitate to use them."

"That's my problem."

"And mine. When you saved me from that boy who was trying to rape me I gave my oath that if you ever needed help I would give it."

"That's silly. It was a child's promise."

"It isn't silly and I never break my word. But it's not only that. If I don't tell Edward I'm your mistress, Miss Wintour will."

"But you're not."

Opal gave a wry smile.

"I think she's capable of contriving evidence to prove I am. People can be bribed to tell lies."

"Surely Kynston wouldn't believe her?"

"I don't think he would, but I can't be certain. Things might never be quite the same between us after that. Perhaps there would aways be a shadow separating us."

"I suppose so. Opal, I want to tell you something but I don't know how to begin. I'm so ashamed."

Opal put her hand over his.

"Now who's being foolish. Old friends don't have to watch their words. What is it?"

"On my way here I prayed you would do as Gillian asks." Campbell got up and began to pace the floor. "I even thought of going down on my knees and begging, though I knew full well I had no right to ask so much of you."

Opal watched him, concerned by the strain on his face. It made him look old and defeated.

"I'm going to lose Edward anyway. Davey, tell me about you and Miss Wintour. It isn't the loss of your business which matters to you, is it? It's because of her promise to go on sleeping with you if we fit in with her plans. I know I ought not to ask, but how can you be so fond of a woman who's prepared to treat you like this?"

It was a second or two before Campbell answered, standing by the window and gazing out as if he were looking into a black abyss.

"It's not fondness; I wish that's all it was. It's hard to explain, but from the first moment I saw her I wanted her so badly that I was prepared to die for her. It's fanciful, especially coming from someone like me, but it was as if she'd bewitched me.

"She isn't just a beautiful body to me; she's part of my soul. Sometimes at night I wake up sweating and terrified because I've dreamt that she's gone away. If I lost her I wouldn't want to live. She's all I want from life. She's mine, and I'd kill to keep her."

It was a Davey Opal had never seen before. A prosaic, down-to-earth man suddenly caught up in something he didn't understand himself. So much passion in his quiet words; such deadly determination. Opal wasn't sure whether it was just a spell Gillian Wintour had cast over Campbell or whether he was half-mad with his obsession for her. She felt a slight shudder run through her as if someone had walked over her grave.

"You frighten me when you talk like that."

"I frighten myself because of my need for her. Still, I have no right to drag you into this."

"I'm already trapped, as I've just said. Don't blame

yourself for my decision, Davey. It was partly to keep my promise, but there are other reasons, too."

He turned his head.

"Oh? What other reasons could there be which are so important that you'd let Gillian do this to you?"

"I don't want the duchess upset. She gave me my first chance when she sent me to Alice Dabbs. She's old and she adores Edward. If a scandal were to break it would hurt her so. I owe Miss Wintour something, too. I became Edward Adare's mistress after he had become engaged to her. It was wrong."

"That was his responsibility."

"And mine. I'm just as culpable as he. I don't want his name sullied by malicious gossip, nor do I want him to be made to look stupid. He would, you know, if all this came out."

"They're not married yet. Gillian hasn't made a cuckold of him."

"She's done the next best thing. Of course people would laugh at him, you know they would."

Davey went back to the settee, sitting beside Opal and looking into her eyes.

"None of the things you've said are important enough for you to take the blame on your shoulders and pretend you're the mother of my bastard. There's something else. Can't you tell me what it is?"

He saw the anguish in her, wishing he could protect her from it as he'd done when they were children, but it was too late for that.

"I suppose you've a right to know." Opal steadied her voice, not wanting to make things worse for Davey. "You see, Edward and I love each other too much, too painfully. I knew from the first that when the time came for us to part it would be dreadful for him. Lately I've seen the sorrow in him and I know he's thinking of the day when we have to say good-bye. When I tell him that you and I are lovers he'll be furious and disgusted, but he'll be free. My admission will kill the love he has for me and lift the burden of it from him. Miss Wintour said she didn't want him mooning over a lost love for the rest of his days. She was right about that. He doesn't deserve such unhappiness. Davey, I've got to let him go – really go for good."

"I understand what you mean, but what of your memories? Can you face the future knowing that Kynston believes you to be a whore?"

"I think so, for him."

"How deeply you must love him."

"As deeply as you love Gillian. Who would have thought that two children from the slums would be capable of such emotions as we feel."

"Dear Opal, you were always plucky but never more so than at this moment. Why couldn't I have fallen in love with you and you with me?"

"It would have been easier, wouldn't it, but it didn't happen. Don't worry about me, Davey, I'll be all right. And don't feel guilty about me either. Remember, I'm not doing this for you, but for Edward. But – "

"Yes?"

She hesitated, trying to warn him.

"Don't let her hurt you too much. She isn't a kind person."

"She's a devil and she'll put me through torment after torment, but I don't care. As long as I can hold her in my arms, touch her lips, stroke her soft skin, I'll manage to survive." He drew Opal towards him, his heart light because Gillian was still going to be his. "Kiss me and tell me you don't hate me because of this."

Neither saw the door open as their lips met, but when they drew apart a slight sound made Opal turn her head quickly.

"Edward! I thought you were coming home to-morrow."

The earl stood motionless, none of the excruciating pain in him reflected on his face. He often laughed at her for going to Belmer Street on her own, but the laughter was full of love. He understood why she had to be there where their happiness lay. It was their private world, shared with no one. Now that world lay in ruins for ever.

"Obviously. I'm afraid I've caused you some embarrassment by my presence. You must forgive me."

Opal felt an icy coldness creeping over her. Edward was a stranger, with blank eyes and thin, unforgiving lips. She knew then that it was over. She hadn't expected the end to come that day or with such shock, but in a way it was just as well. There would be no long days poised on the edge of a precipice, wondering how to make her false confession to him. She wouldn't have to endure a gradual building-up to the ultimate grief. One second of time had done everything for her.

When Campbell rose, trying to explain, she cut him off instantly before secrets could be exposed.

'It's no good, Davey." Opal kept her chin up, not flinching from Kynston's contempt. "The earl isn't a fool."

Edward felt as if he were dying, but he wasn't going to give Opal the satisfaction of seeing that. He had worshipped her, believing she felt the same. He had been wrong. She was just another woman of easy virtue who'd been clever enough to hook a rich man. He refused to let himself think of Regent Street, or the way she had sung and danced outside his house.

Every recollection of their meetings was going to be like a sword-thrust, but this wasn't the moment to weep for a girl who had never really existed.

"Oh yes I am," he said softly. "A bigger fool would be hard to find, but thank you for the lesson. I've come to my senses now and no other woman will ever do this to me. Good-bye, madam, we shan't see each other again. Please leave the key before you go. I don't want this place used as a brothel. The thought is offensive to me."

As the door closed behind Adare, Campbell tried to free himself from Opal's grip.

"You can't let him go like that!"

"Of course I can." She was crying openly now. "That's what we've been talking about. He probably won't give me another thought, but if he does it will be with loathing. I've destroyed the love he had for me because he accepts the evidence of his own eyes. He might not have believed Miss Wintour's story about you and I, but he won't have any doubts about what he's just seen.

"I've done what I said I'd do, but I didn't know just how awful it was going to be. Hold me, please; I'm hurting so much. Oh, Davey, hold me, hold me!"

* * *

Later that night Opal told the whole story to Alice and Herbert Finn, now engaged to be married. She left nothing out, for she had to make them see there was no turning back.

" 'Pon my word, that immoral hussy's worked things out well, hasn't she?" Alice was flushed with indignation. "Surely you don't have to – "

"Yes I do. In any event, as I've just told you, it's partly done already. At least I didn't have to tell him. The earl saw for himself."

"What he saw was a lie. I knew no good would come of you getting mixed up with him. His grandma was right from the beginning. Pity she couldn't have sent you to Timbuktu instead of Whitechapel."

"But she didn't and I don't regret a minute of what I had with Edward. I love him."

" 'Course you do." Finn exerted gentle pressure on Alice's arm. "We're proud of what you've done, aren't we, m'dear?"

"Not so sure that I am." Alice wasn't ready to accept the situation or Herbert's warning. "Self-sacrifice is one thing. This is absurd."

"Not really. I owed it to Davey, and I had to protect Edward and make him forget me."

"What about your career? You could have been one of the greatest stars."

"She still will be." Finn's tone was firmer. "Once all this business is over, Opal will come back here and pick up from where she left off."

"The audiences won't remember her. Out of sight out of mind."

"Rubbish, they'll not forget her. Come on, old girl, let the lass alone. She's got enough on her shoulders without our nagging."

Alice gave up, but not without one last question.

"I expect Herbert's right about people remembering you, but what about the earl? Don't you care what he thinks of you?"

Opal took so long to reply that Alice thought her query had gone unheard. She was about to repeat it, despite Finn's tightening hold on her arm, when Opal said quietly:

"Yes, I care more than I could ever explain to you, but it was nearly over anyway. We only had a few weeks left at most. Dear Alice, it has to be this way. Don't you understand? This is my parting gift to Edward; it was all I had left to give him."

Suddenly Alice melted, moving forward to take Opal in her arms.

"Of course I see and I'm sorry I was badgering you. When the child's born Herbert and I will look after it, poor mite. Then, like he says, you can begin again."

She turned to look at Finn, her eyes moist.

"Herbert, go and get some whisky and don't hurry yourself. Opal and I are going to have a real good cry and we don't need any help from you for that."

* * *

A week after Edward had found Opal and Campbell together he received a letter from Doris Whicker telling him that Annice was gravely ill. The duchess had forbidden her companion to let him know of her condition, but in the end Whicker had ignored her mistress's instructions and put pen to paper.

'She'll be very angry with me when she finds out about this,' Doris had written. 'It can't be helped. I think you ought to come at once, Master Edward, or you may be too late.'

The earl was overcome with self-recriminations. When his grandmother had first told him of her proposed holiday he had been uneasy about it. They were so close that he had sensed something was wrong. For purely selfish reasons he had accepted the duchess's demand that he should remain in London.

He had been glad to obey at the time, wanting to spend every minute he could with Opal. Their love-affair had just started to blossom, and he had turned a deaf ear to the inner voice which murmured warnings about Annie.

At first, the resentment against Opal burned inside him like a corrosive acid, and he welcomed the healthy anger. Then, gradually, his rage gave way to a terrible sense of loss, and he found himself remebering her smile, her kiss, and the way her body had pressed against his own.

At night he dreamed that they were together again, and awoke with a start, her name on his lips. His days were dull and grey because she wasn't there to lighten them for him.

He told his valet to pack his trunks, glad that he was about to put many miles between them. Perhaps the splendour of the Italian countryside would blot out her face and help him to forget her.

He knew he was a fool to entertain such a hope, even for a minute. She would be with him on his journey, still haunting him. He would never be rid of her wherever he went or whatever he did.

A trollop she might be, but he was going to go on loving her until the day he died.

* * *

Two weeks later Gillian Wintour had a miscarriage. Her maid brought a note to *Finn's Music Hall* to inform Opal that her services were no longer required, but that she'd better keep her mouth shut if she knew what was good for Davey Campbell.

Opal was weak with relief because she wouldn't have to play a part in Gillian's heartless scheme. Briefly, she regretted the brutality of her parting with Edward. Then she chided herself for her selfishness. As she had told Davey, Alice and Herbert, a savage break was better for Edward, and he was the one who mattered.

Since the evening when he had walked out of her life she had had to fight misery with every ounce of her strength. She had expected wretchedness, but not its gigantic proportions.

She tried not to think about their time together; to pretend that they had never met. It was a useless exercise, and she flung herself into her work until Alice and Finn protested that she would kill herself unless she took some rest.

When Gillian told Davey the news he was oddly sad. He knew it was stupid to care, for the child would have been deprived of its natural parents, not wanted by its mother. At least Opal's career would not be affected, and that was some comfort to him. It was too late to do anything about Adare, but Opal had said that what had happened was for the best. He didn't dwell on that, not wanting to face the fact that she might have been lying for his sake.

A few days later he was forced to go away on business. He had just acquired some shops in Birmingham, and they needed his personal attention. He didn't want to leave Gillian for three weeks or more, but she calmed his fears.

"Darling, it can't be helped." Gillian was delighted to hear that she was to be rid of Davey for a while. She found him increasingly wearing, and had recently met Lord Rowland Denver, who was shewing a marked interest in her. "I understand why you've got to go and I'm quite all right now. Will you bring me back a present?"

"Of course." He pulled her closer, unaware of the expression in her eyes. "Anything you want."

"You choose. I like surprises."

"Will you be lonely without me?"

"You know I will."

"Kynston's away, too, isn't he?"

"Yes, his grandmother's ill so he's gone to Florence. I detest that woman. I hope she doesn't – "

She saw Campbell's frown and stopped. She wasn't quite ready to get rid of Davey. Denver was rich, handsome, and some whispered that the had a sadistic streak in him. Gillian's heart fluttered when she thought of sharing a bed with him, but nothing had been arranged yet. Davey's money and gifts were not to be thrown away too soon.

"I'm being horrid." She kissed him slowly, watching his doubts about her fade. "Of course I hope she gets well."

"I suppose when the earl's home the date of the wedding will have to be fixed?"

"Yes, it's a bore, isn't it?"

"You'll keep your promise, won't you?"

"What promise, sweetheart?"

He shook her hard.

"Don't tease, not about that. You said we could still be lovers even after your marriage."

"That was when I thought I was going to have your brat. Now – "

"Gillian!"

She threw back her head and laughed in exultation. Maddening though Campbell's possessiveness was, it gave her a very satisfying sense of power over him.

"Swear it."

"Don't be so childish."

"I'm not being childish. I know you and I want your solemn promise."

"Oh God, Davey, not another tantrum." She pulled away from him, wrapping the sheet about her. "Isn't my word good enough for you without swearing solemn oaths? Don't you trust me?"

He knew he had pushed her too far, quick to make amends.

"Yes, yes, I'm sorry. I'm a fool, I know, but I love you so much."

"Then shew it properly. Don't try to make a chattel out of me."

"I won't, never again."

The feline smile returned as the sheet slipped down to her waist.

"You won't, until the next time."

He saw her lips part, thankful that she was done with talking. He had no doubts that he could satisfy her when they made love, for she responded with an abandon which even she couldn't have faked.

That night their sexual pleasure was as good as it had ever been, and Campbell went off on the following morning with a clear mind.

It was when he returned that doubts began to assail him again. He had had to stay in Birmingham a little longer than expected and fretted because of it. His fear grew as he found Gillian had become elusive, taking days to answer his letters and making excuses not to go to their retreat to meet him.

He put up with the situation for as long as he could, but then he knew he had to find out what was wrong. An ugly thought churned his stomach, and his thoughts gave him no peace. A head-on confrontation with Gillian wouldn't serve. She was too good a liar and could talk herself out of anything if it suited her, so he made other plans.

When Jessie Bolt found herself approached by Campbell she sensed no danger at first, pertly wishing him the time of day, her smile saucy.

Gillian hadn't taken long to get Lord Rowland into bed, and her mistress hadn't been as happy or so good-tempered for a long while. The new mood suited Bolt, for when Miss Wintour was contented she was also generous. Dresses, shoes, stockings and even a trinket or two came Jessie's way, and she was very satisfied with the way things were going.

It was only when Campbell hailed a hansom cab and bundled her inside, shopping baskets and all, that she became frightened. Her captor's face was hard as iron, and Jessie knew from Gillian's frequent complaints how jealous he could be. When she tried to protest, Campbell told her to hold her tongue in a way which made her flesh creep. When they reached the house which Campbell had rented, she followed him meekly up the front steps, too scared to make a run for it.

Inside, Davey went straight to the point.

"I want to know why your mistress is avoiding me," he said harshly. "Tell me, or I'll knock the living daylights out of you."

"I don't know what you mean, sir. I – "

Bolt shrieked as Campbell struck her hard.

"The truth and quickly!"

Jessie's eyes were round and stricken, but she summed Campbell up in a trice. It was a full confession or a good hiding, and she saw no reason to protect her mistress at such a price.

Davey listened to the maid's gabble in silence. He knew she was speaking the truth; she was too petrified to do anything else. In any event, he had sensed from the moment of his return that Gillian was up to something. He didn't know who Lord Rowland Denver was, nor did he care. The man had become Gillian's lover; that was what mattered.

"Can I go, sir?"

He glanced at Bolt's tear-stained face.

"Yes. Here's a sovereign for your trouble, and Jessie – "

"Yes, sir?"

"If you mention one word of our meeting to Miss Wintour I shall hear about it and then I'll come and find you and wring your neck."

"I won't say nothin', I promise."

"You'd better not. Now get out of here."

Campbell waited for the door to close and then slowly

mounted the stairs to the bedroom. He went over to the bed with its satin sheets and lace-edged pillows, conscious of the perfume which still lingered in the air.

He had never been one to back away from a fight, and he'd had to do many unworthy things to get what he'd wanted from life. This would be just one more struggle; a passage of arms with a man he'd never seen. He intended to use any weapon necessary to win, for the prize was Gillian and the idea of losing her permanently never crossed his mind.

She'd been unfaithful to him, but she was a harlot by nature. It was no use dwelling on her shortcomings now. What mattered was the, removal of Lord Rowland and Gillian's return to the house which he regarded as a shrine.

"No, my girl," he said as he went downstairs again. "I'm not having this. Maybe you've got to marry Kynston, but you're not going to have any lover but me. I'll see you dead first."

He closed the front door, his face impassive as he signalled to another cabman and made his way back to Kensington to plan his campaign.

* * *

"You should have told me, Annie. It wasn't fair to leave England without a word."

"Fair!" Her Grace's voice was weak but its tone as astringent as ever. "When are you going to learn that life isn't fair?"

Edward looked at his grandmother with troubled eyes. It hadn't been that long since she had packed her bags to go to Florence, but the change in her was dramatic. She was like a tiny doll with a yellowish wrinkled face lined with pain which even she couldn't hide. He took one of her hands in his, very gently, for it seemed so fragile that he was afraid of breaking it.

"I've already done so."

Annice heard the flat note in the earl's voice and turned

her head slightly. If he had found a change in her, she was equally aware of a difference in him despite her slackening hold on reality.

There was the same kind of sorrow in him which she'd seen when she had had to break the news of the loss of his family; the same tribulation which had been so hard for him to fight.

Her vision was blurred, and the dull, dreadful ache was beginning again, but she made one last, supreme effort for Edward's sake.

"You look terrible, Kynston."

He gave a crooked smile. On the threshold of death, Annice was as blunt as ever.

"So do you."

"Maybe, but I'm dying. What's your reason? And don't tell me it's simply that you're grieving about me because I shan't believe you."

"I'm all right."

"Of course you're not. I haven't much strength left. Don't waste what remains of it fencing with me. Said good-bye to that girl of yours, have you?"

"Yes, but not in the way you mean."

"I've no time for riddles either. What happened?"

"I don't want to tire you with my problems. You ought to rest."

"I'll soon get all the rest I need. I wish I had enough stamina left in me to sit up and box your ears for you, you vexing boy. What went wrong?"

At first Kynston spoke so quietly that his grandmother had to urge him to speak up, but when he had finished she gave a snort. It had none of its old fire, but it was as derisive as ever.

"I don't believe it."

"I saw them."

"I still don't believe it. She isn't that kind of woman. Did you ask her why this man Davey, or whatever his name is, was there?"

"I didn't need to; it was patently obvious. She was in his arms."

"But not in bed with him. There could have been some quite rational explanation for his presence there."

"Really! How gullible do you think I am? They were kissing each other."

"Friends do kiss now and then. You're a fool; she loves you. When you go back to England, see her and ask her why the two of them were in Belmer Street."

"No, I can't do that, not even for you."

"Cretin! Still, it's your business and you'll be wed to that tiresome Wintour girl before long. Perhaps it's all for the best."

Her eyes closed, exhausted by her fruitless attempt to make her grandson see sense. Edward was about to rise when she said in a whisper:

"Do something for me."

"Anything, dearest."

"Anything but see Opal Shannon."

"I told you, I can't – "

"All right, it's something else, anyway. Keep an eye on that foolish Doris Whicker for me. I've left her well provided for in my will, but her head's stuffed with cotton. Call on her now and then."

"I promise."

"Leave me now, I think I am rather tired. And Edward – "

"Yes?"

"This may be our last few minutes together. I might not be here in the morning."

"Don't say that."

The whisper grew fainter still.

"Ostrich. I love you, Edward. I've loved you from the day you were born. You've never disappointed me and I know you never will. I wish – "

The earl was near to tears as he bent to kiss the duchess. Annie was right, of course. Death was claiming her even as he watched. He had said another kind of good-bye and it had left him as hollow as turning away from Opal. Things would never be the same again without Annice. She'd always been there to scold, or comfort, or love, and no one could ever take her place.

"I love you, too," he said softly, "and I'll never quite get over losing you. I wish you'd been right about Opal. Oh dear God, Annie, how I wish you'd been right."

Ten

"Well, Miss Shannon? Is my offer acceptable to you?"

Opal was sitting on the edge of her chair in Charles Morton's office, hardly able to believe that she was really there. She hadn't known that Morton was at *Finn's* three nights ago until after the performance. She had almost fainted when a delighted Alice broke the news to her and told her that the great man wanted to see her.

In spite of her deep sadness and her longing for Edward, she had grown better and better at her job. She was a professional entertainer, and the audience wanted to laugh with her, not share the sorrow which would stay with her until she died.

"Yes, more than acceptable." She thrust the thought of the earl away, for Morton was looking at her somewhat quizzically. He wouldn't want an artiste at *The Canterbury Hall* with emotional problems like hers. "I don't know how to thank you for giving me this chance."

"I'm doing myself a favour, not you. You know my motto – One Quality Only – The Best."

"Yes, Mrs. Dabbs told me what it was when she brought me here a long time ago. I loved your baked potatoes."

Morton chuckled. He thought Opal Shannon enchanting and she'd be nothing but an asset to him. Herbert Finn had driven a hard bargain, but it had been worth it.

"Then after your first night I'll serve you with one myself."

"That would be wonderful."

"That's settled then. I'll get my assistant to show you round before you go and will look forward to seeing you next month."

As Opal left the music hall and got into Alice's carriage she let her mask drop. She should have been on top of the world, for she had just achieved her heart's desire. She'd always been sure of her own ability, and this had been confirmed by Ivy, Alice and Herbert. Yet self-confidence and encouragement didn't always spell success. She'd had luck, too, at least in her work, and now the world was her oyster.

She closed her eyes as Edward's face appeared again, stern, disgusted and condemning. She wanted him so much that she didn't know how she managed to get through each day without breaking down, nor how she endured the nights when sleep simply wouldn't come.

She had other worries, too. Davey had also changed, and in a very disquieting way. She could almost feel the tension in him as if it were a tangible thing, and once or twice the light behind his eyes made her fearful. She had tried to talk to him about Miss Wintour, but he'd always been evasive. Her warning that Gillian would bring him nothing but harm went unheeded. Her plea to him to give her up met with no response. She'd visited him only the day before, and he'd seemed more remote than ever, as if he were cutting himself off from other people in order to concentrate on the woman he loved.

"I wish you'd talk to me, Davey," she had said as she poured the tea. "You're bottling things up and that's a bad thing to do."

"It's your imagination."

"No it isn't. Why don't you forget about her? She'll marry the earl as soon as he gets back to England. There's no future for either of you."

"You're wrong." The grey eyes had burned with such intensity that Opal had nearly dropped the cup she was holding. "There'll always be a future for us, she's promised that."

"But what if she doesn't keep her promise?"

"She will, once I've got rid of –"

"Got rid of whom? You mean she's found someone else?"

"She doesn't love him as she does me. She's only doing it to tantalise me, but I'm going to put a stop to that."

After that he had dismissed the subject firmly, but when she left him she was more nervous than before. Davey Campbell had never let anyone or anything stand in his way. There was no knowing to what lengths he would go to keep Miss Wintour as his mistress, nor how long it would be before he started to hate Kynston who was to be her husband.

When she got back to *Barney's Ale House* Alice and Susie were waiting with a hundred questions. She couldn't let them see that Morton's offer was like a burst bubble in her hand, and she assumed a gaiety to match their own as she told them all about the interview and what went on behind the scenes in the music hall.

"I'm so glad for you." Susie hugged her. "Johnny will be, too."

Opal was sad for her and Dibell. The latter had had a hard time at *Webb's* in the Mile End. He'd managed the rôle of the village idiot well enough and had even got a few laughs from the audience. But when the play had ended he'd had to take to shifting scenery, scrubbing floors and becoming a general dog's body to Joseph Webb and his players.

He hadn't complained, and Susie had told her that his weekly pittance was carefully divided between Alice and herself. Susie had started a savings bag, for she intended to marry Johnny in the Spring, come what may.

"There's good news for Johnny as well," said Susie as she put the kettle on. "In a week or two Mr. Webb's going to revive *A Village Tale,* so he will have his old rôle back. I'm coaching him and shewing him some new tricks which he can introduce into the act. He'll be much more successful this time, I know it."

"I'm sure he will, dear." Opal no longer tried to keep her friend's feet on the ground about Dibell. If Susie could wring some comfort from her dreams, so much the better. She knew now how precious even fleeting happiness was and envied Susie and Johnny because their love was still intact and stronger than ever. "I'm very glad for him."

She knew her voice had flagged, conscious of Alice's sharp eyes on her. She had to get away or she would start to cry, and managed a realistic yawn.

"Gracious, I can't think why I feel so tired. I suppose it's all the excitement. I think I'll go and rest for half an hour if no one minds."

She refused Susie's offer to come and help her to remove her best gown, walking slowly up the stairs and leaning against the bedroom door as it closed behind her.

She felt limp, dejected, and a hundred years old. She was about to become a star at *The Canterbury Hall,* but she didn't care a damn. All she wanted was to be in Edward's arms, but that would never happen again no matter how hard she prayed for such a miracle.

Edward Adare had slipped in and out of her life since she was a child, but this time it was different. This time he had gone for good.

* * *

When Edward returned to England he settled Annice's affairs with her solicitors and fixed the wedding date with Gillian.

Gillian had dropped Lord Rowland when she'd heard the earl was on his way home. Rowland was just a plaything; Kynston was going to be her bread and butter, and a great deal more. She and Denver had been extremely discreet, and not even Dulcie Henneker had a notion of what had been going on. If the slightest rumour had got abroad, Dulcie would have been on to it like a hunting dog. Rowland hadn't been troublesome about their parting, like Davey was. Denver had no desire to fall foul of Kynston, and already his roving eye was on the youngest daughter of Lord Merchant.

When Edward left Gillian's house he felt as if he had just had a conversation with a total stranger. Then he realised that's just what she was. He had known very little about Gillian when he had made his rash proposal of marriage. Annice had been right, as always. Gillian was the wrong wife for him, but if he couldn't have Opal one woman was much like another. In any event, there was no way out of the snare he had fashioned for himself.

It was a week later that he found himself outside Pavini's. He wasn't sure how it had happened, for he had carefully avoided going near any place where he and Opal had been together.

As he stood on the pavement he remembered the day he had helped Opal from the hansom, holding her hand and feeling newly-born. The memory was so fresh, as if it was only yesterday that she had bewitched him with her smile.

On an impulse he went inside. The table they had sat at was free, and he took it, having no idea why he was being such a fool. Then he felt a small shock. It was Thursday afternoon and he looked up at the door, his heart turning over.

Opal entered the restaurant thinking about Edward. She often went to Pavini's on a Thursday, sipping tea and going over every word they had exchanged that first day, recalling how their finger-tips had touched on the spotless tablecloth as she had agreed to become his mistress.

When she saw Edward she turned white, unsteady on her feet as she moved forwards. She didn't want to go near him, but something beyond her control was propelling her towards him.

When she reached the table she swayed slightly. Edward rose quickly, instinctively putting out a hand to steady her. Then the anger was back.

"You'd better sit down," he said brusquely. "You're attracting too many curious glances."

"I'm sorry." Somehow Opal found her voice, making much of removing her gloves so that she didn't have to look at Kynston straight away. "If I'd known you were here I swear I wouldn't have come. I thought you were abroad."

"I returned a few weeks ago, after my grandmother died."

"I'm very sorry. The duchess was so good to me. I wish I'd had the privilege of knowing her better."

He hit out savagely.

"She wasn't being good to you; she wanted you out of the way. I was blind to what you were, but she wasn't."

That was too much for Opal. Upset or not, she wasn't going to let Edward bully her.

"It wasn't only that. I won't let you dismiss her kindness in such a way."

"Very well, keep your illusions."

Opal was glad when a waiter arrived with the tray. She could have got up and run out, but that wasn't her way. Fate's hard knocks had to be taken head-on.

"Shall I pour the tea?" she asked coolly.

"Please do."

"I'm told the shortbread here is very good."

"Stop it, damn you, stop it!" Edward's rage was quiet but also deadly. "It's bad enough that we've chosen to come here at the same hour on the same day. You haven't an ounce of shame in you."

Opal bit back a retort, but the earl had seen her reaction and simmered down, remembering how Annice had dismissed his tale out of hand. It was clutching at straws, but worth a try.

"When my grandmother was dying, she told me I should see you when I got back. I didn't want to. Indeed, but for this unfortunate encounter I wouldn't have done so. But, as we're here, I might as well do what she asked of me. She wanted me to find out whether there was something about that night I ought to know; the night I found you with another man in Belmer Street. You called him Davey, I think. So, for her sake I'll ask. Is there anything you've kept from me? Was I mistaken in my judgment?"

The temptation to blurt out the truth and wipe away the look on Edward's face was overwhelming, but Opal gritted her teeth. The road she had chosen was a hard one, strewn with sharp stones and nettles which would prick every step of the way, but there was no turning back now.

"No, my lord, you weren't mistaken."

The glimmer of hope in him died, and he said curtly:

"Then I suggest you finish your tea and leave, unless you want me to do so."

"I'll go. After all, you got here first. But tell me one thing."

He rose as she stood up, wanting to beg her to stay.

"Yes?"

"Why did you come here, on a Thursday afternoon at this hour?"

Their eyes met, and for both of them the chatter of voices and clinking of china faded away. It was as if the world was standing still in order that they should have one last moment together.

Opal wondered what Edward would do if she stretched out her hand and touched his cheek. Edward had to force himself to remember what she had done to prevent himself from pulling her into his arms.

At last the spell was broken, and Opal walked away, not waiting for an answer. Kynston watched her go, turning so that he could still see her as she passed by Pavini's window and out of sight.

Then he sat down again, staring blindly into his empty cup and wishing with all his heart that he was dead.

* * *

Davey Campbell had been drinking heavily since six o'clock and it was now nearly midnight.

He hadn't had to take steps to get rid of Denver; Kynston's return to England had taken care of that.

He had hoped that once Lord Rowland was out of the picture, Gillian would stop avoiding him and ignoring his daily letters, but she hadn't. It was true that twice he'd received a carelessly scrawled note delivered by Jessie Bolt, and once Gillian had come to the house they used, but that was weeks ago.

She made excuses that she was busy preparing for the wedding, or that she had a chill and couldn't go out. He knew she was lying, for Gillian could always overcome difficulties to do anything she really wanted to.

Opal was beginning to irritate him, too. She seemed to call so often nowadays, and the conversation always took the same turn. She would beg him not to see Gillian again, and he, trying not to lose his temper, would refuse. Sometimes he thought Opal was looking at him very oddly, but he didn't ask what was wrong with her. She didn't matter any more; only Gillian was important.

And that morning the final blow had fallen. A letter had come, longer this time, informing him that Gillian wouldn't be seeing him again and that he was to stop pestering her.

'I've tried to make you see that I'm done with you as tactfully as possible, but you won't take the hint, so I'll spell it out plainly. You're nothing but a common lout and you bore me. You amused me once, but not any more. You won't tell Kynston about us and I shan't tell your City acquaintances just what sort of man you are. We'll each keep our secrets, but it's over between us for good.'

Campbell had read the missive fifty times or more, but the message didn't change. Gillian's biting words left no room for hope, no chance of a reconiciliation. The woman for whom he would have given his life was bored with him and wouldn't see him any more.

He rose unsteadily and looked at himself in a mirror. His cheeks were flushed, his hair ruffled. The mouth was a grim line, and the eyes bright as if he had a fever.

"But you will see me again, you bitch," he said aloud. "You'll see me this very night, and then you'll realise how much you still need me. You gave me a promise, and by Christ you're going to keep it."

It was nearly one o'clock by the time he reached Gillian's house. There were no lights on and it was simple enough for one with his experience to find a downstairs window which could be prised open. He knew only too well where Gillian's bedroom was. He had seen her standing at its window, naked and arousing lust in him. In Lockgate he had learned to move about like a wraith to avoid a brush with authority, and the carpeted stairs presented no problem to him.

He crossed to the bed, looking down at Gillian sleeping. She was bathed in faint moonlight, and to him she was still the most perfect woman he had ever seen. Skin so white and soft, dark lashes fanned out on high cheekbones, lips warmly red and made for a man to kiss. He had fortified himself with yet more whisky before he had left home, and it gave him the courage to touch her shoulder.

Gillian awoke instantly, her mouth opening in fear as she saw the outline of a man bending over her. She screamed once, but then a hand cut off her plea for help and there was something heavy on top of her, preventing her escape.

She didn't hear Campbell's urgent words to her not to be afraid; that he had only come to make her see they belonged together. She fought like a trapped animal, and for a split second his fingers slipped and she was able to cry out again.

Her brief attempt at freedom was over and something tight about her throat made her gasp frantically for breath. Still deaf to Davey begging her to lie still, her limbs twisted and turned, her back arched, her nails clawed helplessly at the air.

Then she was quiet once more, as if she was still slumbering. Davey straightened up and lit the candle by the bedside, glad that Gillian had recognised him at last. When he turned his head, terror and disbelief froze him to the spot, and he was suddenly and dreadfully sober.

He was aware that people were running along the corridor outside, but he had no time for them. He was struck dumb by the sight of Gillian's staring eyes. They were like pieces of glass used by doll-makers and they made him shudder.

He made no attempt to escape as Lady Wintour, Bolt and two other servants came rushing in. A long way away he could hear a woman calling out Gillian's name over and over again. Someone mentioned the word police, and he saw Jessie hurrying to the door.

Lady Wintour and the others were shrinking away from him, too frightened to go near the bed. He was hardly conscious of their presence; all he could think of was Gillian. His beautiful, alluring girl who had meant everything to him. He had wanted so much to make her his alone, for it was she who had given him real life, but in the end he had killed her.

At last he came out of his trance, pulling the sheet over Gillian's bare shoulders.

"You were right, my darling," he said softly, "quite right. You said it was over, and it is. Now you'll never belong to anyone but me."

* * *

Johnny Dibell came out of *Webb's* spiritually battered. The revival of *A Village Tale* had only been running for a week, yet already he was receiving the most applause at the end of each performance.

He had no idea why he was succeeding now, when he had failed before. Perhaps it was the help which Susie had given him, or simply the fact that this time the audiences were less demanding.

It didn't really matter one way or the other. His short spell of fame, for he was sure it wouldn't last, had only come to him when he played a half-wit, with hair gummed so that it stood on end, and baggy trousers which kept falling down. People clapped him because he was the idiot, buffeted and knocked about by the other characters in the play, and they felt sorry for him.

Then he saw Susie on the other side of the road, her face lit up with love for him. His frustration and anger melted away as she waved to him. What did it matter how he earned his money as long as Susie was waiting for him when he finished work? They were to be married next month and had already started to look for somewhere to live.

Susie was like a small girl playing mother as she inspected each set of lodgings with great care, running her finger along edges to test them for dust, making sure there were no fleas or bugs.

They had almost settled on a place in Jamaica Street. It was shabby and in need of repair, but the two rooms were clean and Mrs. Rhys, the landlady, seemed a kindly old body.

Webb had given him a rise that day. It wasn't much, but it would buy a pair of sheets and some pillow-cases. He was filled with excitement, longing to see Susie's delight when he told her they were going shopping.

She stepped off the curb, having eyes only for him. She didn't see the heavy brewer's dray, and neither did Dibell until he heard people shouting to Susie to get back. Their warnings were too late, and her scream ripped his mind open as if it had been slashed with a knife.

There were other cries, too, from the women who clustered round Susie and smothered curses from the men who pulled her free of the wheels.

Johnny didn't know how he managed to walk to where Susie lay. His legs didn't seem to belong to him and there was a queer singing noise in his head. He pushed his way through the small crowd which had gathered and knelt by Susie's side. She was like a rag doll drained of its stuffing, and the face which he loved so much was a nightmare now, veiled in blood and distorted like a gargoyle.

Very gently he lifted her and held her against him, murmuring soft words of comfort although he knew she couldn't hear them. When he began to cry, one woman touched him on the shoulder.

"Know her, lad, do you?"

He nodded, still holding Susie fast.

"Yes, we were to be married soon."

The woman and her companions clicked their tongues in sympathy. Death came often to their streets, but this had been a particularly ugly way for a young girl to die.

"My Ted's gone for help; won't be long now. Best you put her down."

Johnny didn't even hear the advice, laying his cheek against the top of Susie's head.

It wasn't only man who had made sport of him; the gods had done the same thing. They had given him Susie and her love and now they had snatched both away.

He remembered her promise to stay with him always, and had a sudden and horrific vision of his future without her. He was so absorbed in his nightmare he wasn't aware that hands had stretched out to take Susie from him and that he was being helped to his feet. Someone had found a reasonably clean kerchief and was dabbing red stains from his shirt and jacket.

No one suggested that he should go with Susie in the ambulance and he didn't ask if he could. He had something more important to do as he lurched unsteadily along the pavement and round the corner to Gibbs Market.

He attracted a few stares, but those who noted his condition assumed he had been fighting and had got the worst of it. They didn't look at his sightless eyes or the tear-stains on his cheeks. He stopped at a stall selling household linen and drew out his week's wages.

"Yes, sir, and what can I do for you?"

Joe Barber who ran the stall thought he'd found himself a rum customer, but he never turned anyone away who had money in their hand.

"I want a pair of sheets and some pillow-cases," said Dibell clearly, as if he had to make the man see how important the purchase was. "Nothing cheap, mind; I want the best. You see, my girl and I are getting married next month. These are to be a surprise for her."

"Congratulations and the best it shall be. Here, look at these; fine as silk. You can tell your young lady they'll last her for the rest of her life."

Johnny focused on Barber's face for the first time.

"For the rest of her life?"

"Aye, for as long as she draws breath. 'Ere, what's wrong with you? Gawd save us, stop it, stop it, you're giving me the willies."

But Johnny Dibell went on screaming with hysterical laughter until finally a constable arrived and led him away, leaving the astonished stall-holders and shoppers staring after them.

* * *

Davey Campbell's trial was brief and without complications. He freely admitted his crime, quite unmoved as the judge pronounced the sentence of death.

He wasn't afraid of the gallows, nor did he want to go on living without Gillian. But he did have one thing to do before the day of execution came and, with the prison governor's permission, he sent a letter to the Earl of Kynston.

When Edward received it he tore it into shreds, filled with outrage. Not only had Campbell killed Gillian, he had been Opal's lover into the bargain.

He didn't know why he changed his mind later that day. Something about refusing a request from a man with so short a time left made him uneasy. It would only take an hour, if that, and then he would be free to continue making his arrangements to leave England.

The trial had been a sensation, for Gillian's relationship with Campbell had been cruelly uncovered for the whole world to savour. Every detail was to be found in newspapers all over the country, couched in words to titillate their readers. The earl didn't want the pity of his friends nor the sly looks, and quickly cut off whispers which followed him wherever he went. He wanted peace and anonymity, and those blessings weren't to be found in his homeland.

When he was shewn into the condemned cell he felt a frisson he hadn't expected. It was a clean room, sparsely furnished, with two warders seated on a bench at one side of the room, Campbell in front of a rough wooden table. At first the place looked quite ordinary, but after a second or two Kynston knew it wasn't. There was an eerie atmosphere about it, as if nothing else existed beyond its walls. In the far corner there was another door, studded with heavy nails. It was hard not to stare at it and wonder what the prisoner would feel on the morning when a key turned in its lock and slowly it began to open.

Then the earl looked at Campbell and found his eyes calm and wholly sane. He was almost cheerful as he asked Edward to sit down, apologising for the uncomfortable chair. It was difficult not to feel some admiration for Campbell, for whatever else he was, he wasn't a coward.

"Well?" Kynston was brief. "I've come as you asked me to. What is it you want of me?"

Davey gave a lop-sided grin.

"Nothing. The boot's on the other foot."

"I don't understand."

"You will when I've told you my story."

"I know your story; so does everyone else. If you've had the effrontery to get me here to tell me how you killed my – "

"I asked you to come so I could talk to you about Opal. Not so long ago I thought she didn't matter to me any more, but I was wrong. She matters quite a lot. Don't start shouting at me; just listen.

"She wasn't my mistress; simply a friend. I'm going to tell you why I was at your house that night and just what Opal was prepared to do for you."

Before the earl could tell Campbell he wasn't interested, the facts were rapped out one by one, concise yet nothing omitted. Of their veracity there could be no doubt, and Edward found himself gripping the edge of the table.

"She was prepared to do that for me?"

"A bit was for me, but mostly it was for you. She loves you as much as I loved Gillian. I suppose you don't think a ragamuffin from the workhouse could really love a fine lady like Gillian, but I did. From the moment I saw her at *Finn's Music Hall* I was damned. I knew from the start that she would be my undoing, but I didn't care. What we shared for a short while was worth anything, even the rope. I didn't mean to kill her; I was trying to keep her quiet."

"I believe you." Edward leaned back in his chair, most of his thoughts about Opal. "There are no barriers where love is concerned. I'm sorry you met Gillian. It would have been much easier for you if you hadn't done so."

"Easier, perhaps, but I wouldn't have missed a second of it, as I've just said. I'll be thinking of her in three days' time when the chaplain comes and starts praying over me. I shan't be listening to him; I'll be hearing Gillian's voice telling me she wanted a master in bed."

The earl said nothing, and Davey laughed.

"Awkward, isn't it?"

"What?"

"Trying to decide what to say to someone who's going to swing. Don't worry about me; it's Opal you should be concerned about. If you'll take some advice from one who won't be around much longer to give it, you'll go to her and apologise for what you accused her of, and then ask her to marry you."

"I doubt if she would agree to do that, or forgive me."

"How little you know about women. She worships the ground you walk on. Why else would she have agreed to do what was asked of her?"

"Perhaps because she's such a good, unselfish person."

"Good God, my lord, what else do you need to convince you of her feelings for you? She said she didn't want the rest of your life spoilt because you couldn't stop loving her. She played the harlot to make you despise her and thus set you free."

"Time's up, m'lord," said one of the warders apologetically. "Sorry to hurry you, but – "

The earl rose, looking down at Davey Campbell, knowing it would be for the last time.

"You're right, of course. Why else would she have done it? I'm afraid there won't be an opportunity for me to pay my debt to you."

"You're not in my debt. It was I who owed Opal something, and now my dues are paid. Look after her, or I'll come back and haunt you."

Edward tried to smile, but it was a poor effort. The room seemed to be closing in on him and there was the smell of death in his nostrils.

"Don't worry, I'll look after her. I love her and I always will. Save your spectral appearances for someone else, Campbell. I'm going to try to make Opal the happiest woman on earth."

* * *

At eight o'clock on the day of Davey's execution Opal buried her head in her hands, saying her private farewells.

Although much had been revealed in court about Davey's *affaire* with Gillian Wintour, the former made sure that she, Opal, did not come into the picture. How he had managed to keep Lady Wintour and Bolt quiet about Gillian's pregnancy, her plans, and subsequent miscarriage, she wasn't sure. Probably he'd used his accumulated wealth to buy their silence.

She wept for Edward as well. How he must have loathed the sordidness of it all. She had tried so hard to protect him, but in the end hadn't been able to stop the mud from sticking to his name. It was in all the headlines – the nobleman who had been duped by a tradesman brought up in the slums. She expected the earl would go abroad as soon as he could, away from the sensation which people would take a long time to forget.

Her mother had once said that sorrows never came singly, and she'd been right. Dear Susie, so full of happiness and love, killed in such an awful way. She had wanted to go to the morgue to see her friend, but Alice and Herbert refused to hear of such a thing.

"Give you the horrors," Alice had said firmly. "You remember her as she was. That's what she would have wanted."

Johnny was in an asylum, and Opal had managed to persuade Alice and Finn to take her to visit him. It had been a dreadful half-hour, with Dibell frothing at the mouth and raving about sheets and pillow-cases.

It was Jed who brought her the large white envelope late in the afternoon. She took it listlessly, half-inclined to ignore it. Then she felt something hard inside it and slit it open with impatient fingers.

She stared at the key; her key to the house in Belmer Street. Then she scanned the note which accompanied it.

'Please come this evening about seven. I won't keep you if you don't want to stay. I went to see Campbell in prison and he told me the whole story. I have some apologies to make.'

There was no hint of affection, and for a while Opal hesitated. It would be painful seeing Edward again, simply to say another good-bye. In the end she put her doubts aside. It was another challenge like The Death Hole. She hadn't shirked that and she wasn't going to weaken now.

Edward was waiting for her when she got to Belmer Street, and they walked together into the drawing-room.

"I know how you must be feeling to-day," he said when they were seated. "You were very fond of Campbell, weren't you?"

"Yes I was." Her voice shook a little. She could still hear the clock chiming eight strokes; a death-knell for Davey. "We went through so much together. When we were in the workhouse he protected me like a brother and that is how I always thought of him."

"I know that now. As I said in my letter, he explained everything to me, especially about that night. I ought to have known Annice was right. She said you weren't that kind of woman."

"Don't blame yourself." Opal knew their time together would be short, but she felt at peace because all the anger had gone from Edward's face. "Any man would have made the same assumption."

"I wasn't any man. I'm the one who would have sold his soul for you. I should have asked what the two of you were doing there."

"No, it's my fault, not yours. When we met at Pavini's you gave me the chance to tell you what happened. I chose not to."

"You did that for my sake, and you'll never know how much it means to me. But for Gillian's death you would have gone on thinking that I hated you."

Opal fixed her gaze on the patterned carpet, not able to look at him.

"You did hate me, didn't you?"

"No." He was studying her beauty and remembering what he had seen in her eyes when he had opened the door to her. It gave him only a flicker of hope, but it was better than nothing. "I was very bitter because I believed you'd tricked me and that I was just one of many men in your life. But it didn't stop me from loving you. I'll never stop loving you."

Opal was afraid to put too much store by what Edward was saying, but there were tears not far away.

"I'm glad about that."

"I didn't write to you earlier. I thought you would prefer to be left alone until after Campbell was – well – after it was over."

"That was kind of you. I wanted to go and see him in prison, but he wouldn't let me."

"He was right to stop you; it wasn't a nice place."

They sat and talked for a while, not only of Davey but about Susie and Johnny Dibell, whose tragic ends had affected Opal so much. She felt Edward's hand over hers, hoping he wouldn't kiss her. It would only add to her sense of loss when he had gone.

"Poor Susie and Johnny. They asked so little of life, but even that was denied them. I dreamed of them last night."

"Don't let your ghosts break you now," he said gently. "You've been very brave. If you want to cry, cry in my arms. That's what they're for."

"I can't. I've got to learn to live without you, and if you held me like you used to do it would make things more difficult for me."

"I see. You're not going to forgive me after all."

"There's nothing to forgive; I told you that. It's simply that – "

"Your Davey said I ought to see you, tell you how sorry I was for being a fool, and then ask you to marry me."

Opal felt her heart leap in her breast, but what Edward was saying was an echo from a daydream.

"Davey didn't understand. You couldn't marry somebody like me."

He laughed as his hand tightened.

"Why not? What is so peculiar about you?"

"You know my background, and now I'm an entertainer on the halls, I'm not a suitable wife for you."

"That's for me to judge. Conventions don't matter to me any more. How could they after all that has happened?"

"There would be even more gossip. You've had enough of that."

"I expect there'll be tittle-tattling in London for quite a while, but I'm going back to Florence, to Annice's villa. We could be married there and start our family. One day, when this is over and forgotten, we can come home if you want to."

She looked at him squarely, ready to take the worst blow of all if she had to.

"Do you really mean it, that you want to marry me? Please don't say you do out of pity or because you think you owe me something. I've had too much to bear already."

He was almost rough as he pulled her closer.

"Pity? Because I owe you something? Don't be ridiculous; you know me better than that."

"Yes, but – "

His anger died as he said softly:

"I want you to be my wife and the mother of my children. If I am to become a whole man again I shall need you with me always. And I love you, my darling, I love you."

Their kiss was both passionate and healing, and it was some while before they drew apart. They smiled at each other in perfect contentment, hands held tightly together.

"Dearest." Opal was reflective. "Do you suppose our room is just as we left it?"

She was very demure, but the look she gave Edward made his blood quicken. He had been so sure that he'd lost her for good, yet now she was sitting by his side offering him what he needed most in the world.

"I expect so," he said, drawing her to her feet. "Do you think we should go and see?"

"It wouldn't take a minute, would it, and it's such a beautiful bedroom."

"It will take a good deal longer than a minute, and you know it, you little hussy. But I'm all in favour of the idea and we've wasted enough time as it is. Come on, Opal Shannon, let's go upstairs and make love."